Memories of the Dead

Phillip R. Hall

Memories of the Dead
Copyright 2011 Phillip R. Hall

ISBN 978-1-105-44185-1

Memories of the Dead

Phillip R. Hall

I used to be envious of vampires. They seemed so delicate, beautiful, and powerful; but now I only pity them, laugh at them. They are so weak and lamentable I wonder now how it could have been that I ever wished to be one.

They are weak because such simple things can injure or kill them--fire, sunlight, lack of blood for food. These are the signs of things that aren't to be embraced but scorned for their pathetic nature. I searched out ages ago to learn about them, only now to wish I had not wasted a single moment of it in such awe of these pitiful beings.

If I assault one with a torch, and set it alight, it burns, it screams, and it either flees and possibly survives, or it dies where it once stood. But me, if you burn me, my flesh will render, yes; but I become much more than I was! As my body burns, my massive will keeps me animate, and as my body dies my power increases. Even to the point where there is no flesh on my bones, I live still; and should, through the long eons of time, my bones disintegrate into naught but dust, I remain forever potent. As I dissolve I become more powerful, and violence to me only hastens the process.

They control the darker creatures through the repugnance of

mind control. Ha! To control the minds to weaker beings is nothing to be impressed with. I can do the same, and have many times; yet it is simpler and just as effective to use what normal guile man has on another--threaten, cajole, buy a man's loyalty with wealth or promises. Where they hide themselves away from the world, lest they be found out, I revel in the life of men--the seething and brooding of the populace. They need not fear me; I do not bring death to their doorstep. I only wish to exist among them for all time, and have them with me-- near me. In a manner of speaking, I have come to think of the living as my pets. I watch them, take enjoyment from their company, play with them; but they are not my food, nor are they a broken family to which I desperately cling as a reminder of a former life.

Whereas their souls are damned, mine is not. I did not give up my existing spirit to some infernal power to become what I am. To the contrary, I know exactly where my soul is: it is protected by powerful means, encased in a phial where, at any moment, I can reclaim it, marvel at its light, or consume it and be reincarnated again as a mortal being. If there is a weakness to this existence of mine it is this: I need protect my soul-in-a-jar from the ravages of other men. Should they come to possess it, they could destroy my spirit and my existence with it.

Though I live still, when this mortal body dies I will continue on; and shall rise up, even in that very moment, a being of unsurpassed power. Were it to happen quickly, one might not even see it come to pass. All the preparations are completed, the soul-transfer is done, and the phial is full, sealed, and hidden. All I need do now is wait out my life, live it as I choose, how I choose, and with whom I choose, until the last breath leaves my lungs. Then I will be made anew.

I will be undead at that moment, and that is the only thing I share with those bloodsuckers, but I will be something more than they can imagine. Something terrible to behold, something wonderful, something the world cannot truly understand.

I learned the craft years ago when I studied at the scholarly hands of a coven of like-minded men and women who wished to learn what true sorcery remained in the world. Being an altruistic group, they used their gained knowledge to assist those in dire need--I along with them. Some powerful spells were considered unnatural, and they shunned their use--some things were meant to be left alone, they would inform me. These are the things I wanted to know.

In the dark nights we studied ancient tomes written by people long lost who learned what real power was--what it meant to be able to move mountains and bring down stars from the sky. But in my opinion, just because a ritual provided life beyond death did not make it some kind of anathema--forbidden --damned--to be avoided. All things have a place under the dome of creation, these too, else it would not exist.

What I will become originates from, I am told, the ancient German word for corpse. But a mere corpse I am not, nor will I be. What I am should not be confused with a zombie, which is a soul-less, animated, dominated thing that scurries; I am my own master, and none can command me as zombies are. I am not (as I have said) a vampire, for they are but parasites living off the lives of others all the while moaning their sad tale of immortality to any onlooker who would hear.

I am a *Lich*. And through the dark centuries to come I will be more powerful than a thousand vampires. Even though only a few of those worthless bottom-feeders exist, they are strong; but of my kin there will be only me.

I am Locarno, and this is my tale.

Now, just because I have prepared myself for my eventual demise, don't get me wrong--I am not trying to die, nor am I rushing headlong into it. I simply had the fortune to find that there was a way to postpone what happens to a person when their body stops living. I am no masochist, and I don't think I'm stupid; merely prepared for the inevitable.

Perhaps I should start where it all began. Back when I was twelve, I had visited my Grandfather in his home on the outskirts of town. He was a lovely man, with blue eyes, a beard that was speckled gray, the last remnants of the color his hair used to be; and he had a quite pleasant demeanor. Having served in both the military and as a minor court official to His Majesty, he had acquired a bit of a small fortune--along with trinkets from the far-flung world. Most of these baubles he kept in a cedar trunk in his library.

But the most valuable things he had weren't made of wrought silver or pounded gold, no: they were his books. His library was well stocked with impressively large works from all over the world--some in French, some in German, some Latin. Each of them was, to me, a marvel, ornate and beautiful. Truly something the enlightened had mastered.

At that age I was nearly a man and in a few years I would be considered such; but yet I could not read the words on the illustrated pages. At the time it was commonplace for most everyone to be illiterate; and when I showed interest, that's when he taught me the beginnings of how to read.

Slowly, obviously, and in English first, with smatterings of the others here and there, I made progress toward understanding--and toward who and what I would become. Once I made the mental adjustment to understand what was there on the page, rather than just mimicking the word-sounds, I understood that these books weren't just "lessons in history," as he put it, but were something quite more. He knew that I understood. The books were filled with euphemisms that were needed to protect yourself from those who are keen to probe your secrets for their own gain--or your suffering--these two are tied to one another inexorably.

Grandfather was a practitioner in forbidden arts, as I would learn. But he wasn't a witch--that was a word too easily thrown around by those that don't know the true meaning of it. No, he was a plain man who knew a few secrets--he could do a few remarkable things that ought not be possible--but he was otherwise just as you or I in everyday life: he would go to the garden and harvest vegetables (potatoes were his favorite), to the market to buy meat or cloth, and occasionally he'd chop wood for the fire (but usually he'd have one of the elder children in the vicinity do it, have one of our relatives help, or make me perform the work.)

He was just as you would expect an elderly man to be, but he was much more than that. He was a great friend, and of all the people in the world, I think he was the best possible person. His laugh was like running water to a parched plant. He was quick to correct, but never stern--he took a very active interest in my reading progress. As I devoured the books, page by page, and learned what was truly going on he would explain, produce examples, teach me to replicate the effects and perform what some might call minor miracles.

As I learned more and more, and the number of books in his library that I had not read and memorized were reduced to but a handful, and as my own mystical capabilities grew practically exponentially (a word he taught me along with the workings of numbers he called mathematics), we came to his final lesson.

There was one book, a large black one, that he said I would be wise from which not to read, nor practice that which was contained therein. It was, as he put it, "The Book of Death," and the contents were things his group--to whom I had been introduced as a new acolyte--considered (and they used this word quite sparingly) evil.

(Now a word about his group: no coven were they. No witches practicing dark blasphemies or corruptions of the Holy Mass; no perverse outbreaks of wickedness would be found among them. They were educated and elite; they thought only to better the lives of mankind, using their prowess, influence, wealth, and status to help those in the direst of need. However, were they to be discovered, it would be a calamity--prison or perhaps execution. Sorcery was, as explained, quite a serious matter with which to be involved. Therefore, each member was sworn to secrecy, and with these people their word was their bond--it could not, nor would not, be broken.)

The book was thick, perhaps as long as my littlest finger, with black leather (skin, perhaps?) cover and a binding. No marks were on it otherwise; it was plain, really. Perhaps it was its apparent plainness that drew me to it initially. I waited for a time when I could peer into the book, behold its wonderment, and learn the last of the knowledge that Grandfather had available for me. But he was often home, and I would simply have to wait for a time when he was not.

I do not wish to sound overly rebellious. I know my grandfather well, and understand that he wished only to protect me from things that might be appalling or dangerous to me; but to hold out a thing to a child and say "This thing you may not touch," then only to put it on a shelf where it could be grasped is really asking for the worst to come into being. That book was magnetic toward me, it filled my dreams, my thoughts conjured up visions of what might be within it-- what secret was too unholy to not reveal?

But that would take guile and time to unleash.

Over the next two summers I practiced my art, with Grandfather always there--ever at the ready to lend a hand--to give advice or to help me get out of a situation that went mildly out of control. One would be surprised at how easily that sorcery can get you in trouble if your attention falters for even a second. I remember conjuring a simple bolt of flame, in an attempt to ignite a small log out at his wood-shed, when I heard a noise, turned only my head to see what it was (a woodpecker rustling through leaves, I know now), and managed to nearly ignite half an acre of dry pasture.

Something you may not know about sorcery is that you can conjure up almost anything you can imagine--with patience and practice--but whatever you do will be blatantly unnatural; so the mystical impetus you have must come to an end, but the effects might linger on. I was making that flame, and when I stopped, the fire still burned what fuel was there. In order to quench it I had to either contain it until it expired or produce a counter effect.

Water serves nicely for most fires, of course. Luckily, there is a well on the property, and a bucket. Could I have conjured up rain or some other power to end the fire? Yes, but sorcery takes time, and fire is greedy and swift. Additionally, the tools--all I really needed--were at the ready. It is almost as if Grandfather knew something was going to happen: he was often quite prescient.

He told me I needed to be a bit more careful next time, laughing, that was all. He was there the whole time, perhaps it was sort of a test in a way, to see what I could do--what I would do--if something went dreadfully wrong. I think I passed pretty well, all things considered; but I learned that destructive power is something that you should have a healthy respect toward and that you should always pay close attention to your works.

After that I spent a lot of time honing my will, and I got to the point when I was performing any duty I was nearly unshakable from it until I knew it was safe to let my mind wander to other matters. I found I was remembering things more easily as well; and I had less and less need to reference any of the books from his library. He marveled at my ability to memorize them completely, I just thought I was being more focused. But apparently I had a gift for it.

In all this time, Grandfather never strayed from his home. Two years and more, I was there daily, learning, helping, performing menial acts around the home (cooking and cleaning, usually)--payment for the knowledge he was bestowing upon me. I actually enjoyed it a lot. Grandfather was more of a friend than mentor, and certainly more of a father-figure to me than my own parent--who was off with the militia more often than not; and when father was available he was never at home. Still to this day I do not understand why someone would marry, begin a family, and then in some debased form of abandonment leave them mostly to their own devices. Mother was lucky, I suppose, to have a husband at all, seeing as there were plenty of pretty young girls around trying to obtain a bridegroom. Despite not having a dowry, they vied against one another quite fiercely. Even I, as a young man, had the affection or attention of at least one at any moment. But I wasn't ready for that. I had better lessons to learn. I ignored the attentions of girls.

Each night, I felt the black book call to me from across the night air, beckoning me to come probe its pages. Every night, I dreamt of what (I thought) must be in it--what there could be--what majestic insights into the very nature of Creation itself! But Grandfather never left home long enough for me to see it.

Every morning, while I prepared breakfast for us both, almost like clock-work, Madame Beck would come to visit. Dressed in what shabby finery she had at hand--clearly, she was once a wealthy person, or obtained the garments from someone who was long ago able to care for them more properly--and she would stay with him in the library for no more than a few moments with the door closed.

At first, I thought she and he were having an affair or conjugations; the idea was exciting to me--that a man, nearly at the end of his life still had such strength! But alas, that was not what was happening: I had crept to outside the door on a couple of occasions, out of curiosity and titillation to discover they were only talking. I couldn't hear it all, but it was a usually little frantic on her part, with hushed reassurance that I knew so well from him. Something was definitely wrong, but I couldn't tell what. She was a paranoid.

I had to be careful, I didn't want them to know I was prying into their personal conversations, but being still a child I was curious (and not at all malicious) about the situation. I remember one such meeting of theirs particularly well. She came, as usual, and I greeted her, as usual; but she was distraught mightily, even more so than usual, nearly in tears. She rushed in almost before I could announce her coming and headed straight for the library.

Grandfather met her there at the door (he was already within). In their haste, they didn't close the door. I strained to listen, but with her in such an agitated state I heard relatively clearly. And the words I heard were quite chilling.

"Doctor Weld is dead!"

Doctor Weld is...was...a physician and apothecary where we lived. A well respected man, intelligent, a little gaunt, elderly, not feeble, and kind. He was more notable to me specifically because he was one of Grandfather's inner circle of friends--a fellow practitioner of sorcery. I had met him on several occasions. He'd come to the house, inquire as to how my studies were progressing, and have me perform a trick or two, smile greatly and say "Splendid!" (That was his favorite word to use when he was amused or pleased.) I liked him a great deal. But now, he was dead.

I assumed he died of a physical condition, or perhaps was attacked by an animal (a wolf or two had been seen nearby not long ago. It's hard to tell, two wolves might appear as one in the distance.) My prayers for him that night would be most heartfelt.

Grandfather asked Madame if she knew how he died, "It must have been something he ate?..."

He was good as that: probing with questions that weren't really questions. Truly, he was able to obtain information like no other.

"No!" She nearly cried then, "He was killed!"

"Killed? Nonsense!" Grandfather blotted out the idea. "Are

you sure?" Realizing that she wouldn't lie to him.

Over the next few minutes she told him what she saw, what she knew, and how she knew it; pausing only to break down into tears once or twice. The question I wanted to know was the same as Grandfather, only he dared to intone it aloud: "Why would anyone want to kill Herbert Weld?"

"I don't know," came her slight reply. "But I do know this: he had a mark on him."

"Oh?..."

I knew that tone of his voice; it meant we were going somewhere--very soon.

"Locarno!" He called for me.

At first I wasn't sure if he knew I was listening, but soon it became clear he didn't.

"Locarno! Get in here quickly!"

I shuffled in, just past Madame as she left--who knows where she was off to, but it didn't really matter.

"Listen, I have some bad news," he began. "The Doctor is dead..."

He then went on to tell the tale I already knew, but having already known it didn't change the impact it had upon me. I was still stunned, silent, and more than just a little shaken. I had barely any time to let it all sink in and he started again.

"We're going! Come!"

Where we were going was clear: to the Doctor's home. Grandfather wanted to know what happened, how he died, and if there were clues to it all--and of course, that mark on him that Madame saw--all of it added up to something. We just didn't know what.

We hurriedly went through the side streets to the Doctor's home. Getting there wasn't hard, we both knew the way, but the dew in the morning air made the trek a little cold; and by the time we got there I was damp, chilled to the bone, and still hungry as we hadn't yet eaten.

Going inside, I was surprised at how dark the place was.

Usually he had candles lit everywhere--somehow he always managed to find the biggest ones--but now the fire in his hearth had long since diminished to mere embers.

We found his body at his desk, thrown to the side, facing the window--the window Madame must have peered into when she saw him--with his chest was barely covered by his night-shirt. There was dried blood around his mouth, and some under his fingernails; but otherwise, there were no signs of a great scuffle. Whatever had happened, it had happened quickly.

I had never seen a dead body before. At first I was a bit sickened at the sight. This was a family friend--almost family himself--and that only made it all the more worse. Death was right there--in front of me--personified in the corpse of a man who not two days earlier I had spoken to and shared a small meal with. This man, this friend, soulless in his last repose, was without the spark of life he had shared openly with me. I was aghast. Had there been more time, I think I might have cried or at the very least been sad, or at the very least been sadder than I was.

But there, beneath and barely covered by his shirt was the mark; and it was just as Madame had said.

It looked to me like a black flame burned into his chest, about an inch high, near the heart. I pointed it out to Grandfather. Unceremoniously, he opened the shirt, and we then saw that what I had perceived (and what Madame saw) was only a small part of yet a larger branding.

Yes, the good Doctor has been branded: like cattle. I could smell the slight acrid odor from the flesh it burned. The pain must have been horrid. The design was like that of a sunrise of a black sun, the lower half missing as if hidden by the flat horizon, and above the semi-circle, five flames evenly spaced. The whole mark was perhaps four or five inches across at best and maybe just as tall.

When Grandfather saw it, he stood back and was, I think, genuinely frightened. So much so that as he did, he let something slip from his lips (very unlike him), and I heard it.

"...*Dies Irae*..."

I knew enough Latin to know what those words meant--"Day of Wrath"--but what significance they had I did not (yet) understand.

And almost as quickly as he said them he blurted, "Come! We're leaving now!"

"But what about the Doctor? We can't leave him like this!"

Yes we could; yes we did, and we went. Grandfather was nervous, agitated, fidgety, and looked behind him frequently along the way. This was all unlike him; that alone made me as nervous as he. Luckily, we made it home again safely, for it seemed none had followed us--but what we did not know at the time was that we were watched by eyes unseen; and now they knew that we were aware of what had transpired, but we were blissfully unaware of their attentions.

Immediately upon entering our home, Grandfather began to shutter the windows, which was odd as he always liked the sunlight to come through, being one who dearly loved the outdoors. Then he said something I knew was ominous just from how he said it.

"Throw more wood on the fire."

The hearth was already glowing from earlier, although the fire had gone down quite a bit, the breakfast we never managed to get to was now boiling quite furiously--and I was about to load it up with more wood at his request. While I did that, he disappeared into the library and he quickly came back with armfuls of texts and papers.

He was sweating, breathing heavily, but in control.

"We need to burn this. All of it."

I looked over what he had as I took some of the burden from him, some of it was silly things that might be heretical, best if those were burned first; also he had all his mystical texts, and among those was one I knew all too well: the black book.

The fire had leapt up greater, and was more amenable to burning paper than before. Now it seemed that I would not have the opportunity to peruse the last volume of hidden lore, and I was a bit sunk by the thought, and it must have shown.

"My boy, don't worry. With these out of the way things will be safer."

He told me to begin the burning and wait for him when all was ashes. He had "One thing yet to do," and he left quickly, as if in a daze.

Dutifully, I began tossing papers into the fire. I'd open one, look, see if it was important, become a bit sad, then consign it to the flames. It wasn't long before I got to the last--the one I hadn't read--the book that filled my dreams.

I, at long last, held the book in my hand. That's when a curious idea came to me. The book would be burned, but its secret knowledge would not be lost.

I took from the black binder the pages and ripped them out. They removed from the sewn bindings easily--the age of the book played a major part in this, no doubt--and replaced them with other pages from the pile to be destroyed, and put the binder onto the top log in full blaze. The pages from it I sequestered to my room, and shoved them into the straw and down padding on which I took my nightly slumber. Hidden, I thought, well enough, and would remain there for me protected until I could retrieve them again.

I walked back, perhaps a little smugly, but mostly nervous, to the hearth. The binder of the black leather was so badly burned now you barely knew that it was a book at all. With the rest all burned or smoldering to ash, I waited for Grandfather to return and did what any sensible person in this situation might do: I ate the long awaited breakfast, sat, and worried about the morning's events and what next may transpire. What caused me concern was the Latin *Day of Wrath*, which I knew only basely--a poem about the end of times, when God would judge man for their sins. What that had to do with the Doctor, I simply could not puzzle together.

The timing apparently could not have been better, just as I had begun to relish my food and bread, Grandfather came through the door.

"Did you finish?"

I pointed to the fire, all was ablaze, and he was contented at that.

"Good!" And as he sat, "I went to tell Simm, the Younger, to be watchful, wary, and that something was afoot. He asked few questions, as usual."

He followed by "Is there more of this?" while motioning to my plate.

About Simm, the Younger--I never liked him; he was quiet, odd, and elusive. Lugubrious and seemed to not appreciate either the gifts or wealth he had or the simpler life afforded to him by living here. He was altogether not the kind of person you want to be around for long as his cynicism and dismal nature seemed to carry over to those near him. All in all, he was a person whom you would consider the polar opposite of Grandfather; and why they were friends, I have no Earthly clue.

Regardless, I prepared him a bowl quickly with some bread. When I turned to give it to him, that's when he began again. He told me *Dies Irae* wasn't just some poem, but rather a way to oblivion. Long ago, a faction of the Church had split from the core. Where the mainstay belief was one of repentance and remission of sin, *Dies Irae* believed that Man was unworthy of redemption and that apostasy, greed, sin, lust, and lack of true faith had doomed Man; and that God had turned his back on us--there was no recourse, no remorse, and no forgiveness forthcoming. They believed that it would be better for Man to die out than to live in such misery; as such, *Dies Irae* had dedicated themselves to--starting with people of knowledge, power, wealth, and status--the reduction of Man from civilized to barbarism, and in the ensuing chaos that would reign, God would have no choice but to disavow his creation and to start fresh.

"*Dies Irae*," he continued, "Wished to hasten the coming 'Day of Wrath' and destroy all that had been built. Civilization, knowledge-- all these things were not the native state of Man and we did not deserve them; and that God must wipe clean the slate of Creation."

Their lot was one of suffering and death. These were the people responsible for killing and branding our good friend, my mentor, the Doctor--and they had come to our very doorstep. The Day of Wrath had begun by destroying the halcyon days that existed just moments ago.

Perhaps I should be clear: just because Simm, the Younger, was the way he was, that didn't mean I hated him in the way most would understand the word--in some detestable manner--rather, he was, simply, someone with whom you just couldn't get close--you could never get to know him well. He was, in many ways, some kind of sad enigma. He had wealth, courtesy of his father's status, a modicum of fame (coming from an important family will do that to a person); and had the attentions of practically every girl in the region, except, for obvious reasons, his sister, Juliana.

It is as if everything he had or was given--all the gifts that his nearly noble birth-right had provided him--were meaningless. He was austere in every sense and definition of the word. Perhaps he just needed a little more age in him, like a bottle of wine not quite ready to be enjoyed.

Though I was used to it, having been around him and his father--as they too were acquaintances of Grandfather--I got the distinct feeling that he would have rather been an ascetic or a monk. He spent a great amount of time at the local abbey with the pious that resided there. I think he found the surroundings serene, peaceful, and may have reinforced to his mind that there was orderliness to the universe, and that all was not truly chaos, though it may seem such.

Sometimes, he would go on about how frail humanity was and that had it not been the grace of our Savior all those ages ago we would have fallen into self-carnage and misery with precious little to keep us from our own destruction. But at other times, usually when he had just returned from the abbey, he was more delightful--and became a tolerable person for at least a little while.

So he wasn't utterly depressing and mournful; but I would not, as I said, had even stood to be near him if it weren't for two important factors: one, his father was a member of my Grandfather's inner circle of friends; and two, his sister was quite lovely to look at--even though I had chosen to steel myself to my studies I was still, after all, a man; and the desire to view an attractive young lady, as Juliana was, is something altogether native and innate to our being.

Grandfather knew that I was, in a way, smitten with her; and after a time I didn't even need to prod him for any new news about her. I think it pleased him to know that I was interested, even though I never knew if she was at all aware of my affection.

The day of the Doctor's murder went as much as any other day would go: chores, cooking, lessons, talking about the day, although the talk this day was more sad and reflective--and a bit paranoid. Nobody came to visit the remainder of the morning or the afternoon; but early evening there was a visitor, and when the knock came it startled us both.

There was a constable with tall helm and wearing leather and ring armor at the door, and another beside him dressed similarly. The one to the rear I casually knew as he was a friend of my father. Apparently, they had served at the front together some time ago. We exchanged pleasantries and then they began to explain why they were at our door. They had come to talk to Grandfather about the Doctor's death--which by now had become known to the authorities--how exactly, it is unknown (I always suspected Madame had told someone else and they informed the local militiamen.) We were questioned for a bit, but Grandfather's word was binding, having been an honorable man; they also knew he was no liar--and certainly no murderer.

We told them what we knew, how we knew it, and when (and from whom) we learned it--but were careful to leave out any mention of the branding. When asked why we didn't report it directly when we were aware of the Doctor's death, we took no pause to answer: we were not used to such sights and were afraid ourselves, and fled.

True enough. I still was worried that whoever did this--this *Dies Irae*--might next come to us. The look on my face alone may have sealed it for the militia; they looked at me, nodded in agreement, and then bid us good evening and left.

Grandfather shut and bolted the door behind them. It then seemed that, other than the fact there was some crazed madman in our midst, the worst of it was over. He explained that *Dies Irae* tended to appear swiftly, perform their acts of terror, and disappear just as quickly as they came; and that they were few in number.

From the militiamen we learned that as there was now no physician in town there would be little reason to examine the body more exhaustively, as none had the requisite skill to do so; therefore, it would be marked as a murder, by an unknown assailant, and that the funeral would be in a day--provided the spring weather held clear and that a suitable grave could be found. It would not be an exaggeration to say that the militia wanted the problem to go away as easily as possible and didn't actually wish to investigate more than necessary. The authorities in a locale such as this are often the most self-serving of individuals, and compound this with their lazy nature one obtains clear indication that they wish only to be paid and to do very little (or as little as possible) to get it.

It was here I came to believe that although it was valuable to have such defenders of the public around; one shouldn't count on them to do that for which they are employed. Justice, it seems, could be easily delayed when lack of care or mindlessness reign; and that sometimes, justice was something that needed to be taken and not given.

As the evening progressed, I retired to my room, where I knew that the hidden documents lay in waiting for me. Withdrawing them from the bunk, I pulled seemingly random pages, from which I needed to reorganize them correctly--which is no easy task, as the pages were not numbered.

Once re-collated, I began at the beginning, which seemed the appropriate place. Within the confines of the book there were only a few actual items; first was a process by which one could commune with the recent dead, provided the body was available--this should serve a valuable purpose one day--but there was an admonition that the dead are best left to lay where they are, undisturbed and unquestioned, for they are known to lie to further the goals they once had in life, and therefore were not entirely trustworthy, and man can be easily misled.

Truth to be told, I was still quite concerned about the day's events and wasn't completely in the mood for the knowledge that I once had striven and yearned so longingly to peruse. I was afraid, and kept with me while I slumbered a large cleaver that I took from the kitchen--for defense should someone come for me as had the Doctor. Reinserting the pages to my bedding, more carefully and in order, I endeavored to find rest.

My sleep was fitful; the howling of wolves could be heard that night, and quite loudly. I am not sure where these animals had come from, but they were near now, and more than one as far as I could tell. Perhaps they would act in some form of warning should someone or something else approach? I could only hope that would be true. It was rare to see wolves (or in this case, to hear them) this close to our home. Hunters, no doubt, will be out after them in the morning. Dangerous, too dangerous they are, to be allowed any sort of free-reign around people or livestock.

This night, when I slept, I dreamt about Juliana. It was, when I did dream of her, always the same: there she sat on a throne, adorned in mink and sable, wearing a crown of gold; and at her feet were two children--infants--and she wore expensive finery. She was happy. I looked at her as if from on the other side of a door or perhaps from a framed window. She would see me, and smile more greatly. Like a torch, her hair and smile would light the room which was otherwise black and totally obscured.

I do not know why she was in this fashion in my dreams, but this is how she was seen. We never spoke; and the noises I heard were only that of the children at her feet, cooing as only a baby can. Perhaps this was my seeing her as something unobtainable or purposefully set aloof? I had no idea, and never did understand it. Presages of things to come, perhaps? For years, or at least as long as I could remember, when I dreamt of her, this is how I always saw her. Each time after I awoke after such a dream, I wished I had gone through the portal to her, and at least spoke with her, or touched her, or held the babies--something.

But I never moved, never wavered. Perhaps one day I will force myself through, if for no other reason but to drive the dream forward. Being stuck like that, in the repetitive events of this particular dream, is a little frustrating.

I awoke just enough to roll-over; I heard the wolves again,

and wished they would be silent. Stupid animals have no common decency to remain silent when people are trying to rest. I know that is a vanity that only men have, and it really is unfair to blame the animals for their being themselves, but sleep we must have, and silence is required; and wolves, if they so wish to remain wild or alive would do well to respect men and not to draw near to their dwellings, and certainly to remain quiet when doing so. It is not that I mind animals, they have their place and so do we; simply that I wanted sleep more than I wanted them to act in any fashion as ordinary. Petty, I know, but I am a man, and that is how we act on occasion.

I fell asleep again, reaching out from my bed. I felt something warm and fur-covered brush my hand. I felt hot breath on my fingers, and I heard a growl.

I tightened and slowly I grabbed my cleaver, I hoped it would be enough. If a wolf had come into my room, I would need it to be sharp and I would need to be quick to defend myself against the claws and teeth of a beast nearly my size or larger. I could hear its pulse, or so I thought. My eyes still closed, my breathing was hard. If animals can truly taste fear, then this one would have a savory meal that would last days.

I was afraid to open my eyes. My hand was still exposed, and were I to pull it back I may find myself bitten. I thought quickly and came up with a plan I felt was acceptable: the next time I felt the brushing on my fingers I would scream and attack. Otherwise, remain still and wait. Brilliant, I mused.

I waited, listening, I heard it. I felt nuzzling at my fingers. Closer! I wanted it just a little closer so as to grab fur that my hands might not miss with the (perhaps) only swing of the cleaver that I might have. I swallowed hard. Breathing laboriously, I waited. Closer! Please closer or flee!

Again, I felt the body, warm and loose against me. It was now the time to act on my conviction. Fear nearly griped me and made me stone. Oh, let this work!

I grabbed with all the strength my fingers had left! Strongly, and it pulled back. I yelled, opened my eyes, and raised my arm with cleaver to strike.

And there, before my wild-eyes was Grandfather standing. My fingers on his over-wrapping cloak, and his eyes twice as wide as mine!

"Locarno!" He screamed, "It's me! Awake!"

I was in shock, just breathing and amazed. Grandfather! Thank heaven!

"What is going on with you?" He asked, pulling my fingers from his coat.

"Wolves!" I said.

"Wolves?" he replied, "Yes, outside. You were dreaming just now."

It was morning and the sun was already high. I had slept, deeply indeed. Gathering ourselves, and our remaining dignity, I began to get dressed properly. Usually, I am up before he, and I apologized.

"Well, no harm done," he puzzled, "But I must ask, what kind of wolf do you know that can open a bolted door, hmm?"

I had no answer, just a blank stare. He laughed. It was morning, and there was much to do and it was time to be about it.

The day was brisk, and uneventful. I had worried, and was still a bit upset from the dreams previously; but that faded in time as the day wore on. I expected more visitors, knocks with portent on the portal, if you will--but none came, thankfully.

Chores were done, dinner was simmering, and I even had a small chance to train a bit more with Grandfather. I levitated a chair for a brief moment. It was exhilarating!

As I did so, I was told that manipulating a living (or formerly) living thing is far easier than something that never lived. Living things know how to move and sway and grow, and formerly living things have almost a memory in them of how to move, so they are more apt an object for such manipulations. It is the tiny morsels of great wisdom that Grandfather had that I enjoy learning--none of the texts he had ever mentioned that wood would yield more so than iron.

It is true that iron--or for that matter, any metal--can be made to respond to mystical commands, just that it takes greater effort. When Grandfather was not looking, I tried to move my iron spoon. It moved--barely--but it moved. I would have to work on that to gain greater effect.

Plants respond to sorcerous calls easily, as do some animals--they can be made to do one's bidding, and if you have the talent, you can even communicate with them. Grandfather couldn't actually instruct me on that, as he claimed no such ability amongst the powers he held. Pity.

I had a few moments to myself outside, and I saw a squirrel scampering about and thought it a good test to see if I could call it to me. I wanted to see if I could commune with it, but it just kept on searching for nuts and food, paying me no mind. Apparently, I don't have the talent for animalism either. But with plenty of people around, I really don't know what a forest animal might have to offer me in conversation that I can't obtain from one of my neighbors. I convinced myself that there are some things about the life of a squirrel, or a bat, or a cat, or a dog that I really don't find myself wanting to know. More vanity, perhaps, in my failure than I care to admit.

Grandfather came out--finally--and we were off. The Doctor's funeral was today. He was our friend, and therefore deserved our last measure of loyalty. I hated funerals just as much as death; I will miss him, but I didn't want to go--forced to stand for seemingly forever just so we have the opportunity to wish him well in the afterlife--something I can do from my stoop and need not travel (even the short distance) to do. But it is ceremony that people like: order and form. So we go and the meaningless pomp begins.

The process of funerary rights isn't much different anywhere you travel--a church service and a brief moment in the sun culminating the burial of the loved-one. I don't remember much of the procession in the church because I was distracted--Juliana was there.

She sat before us; I could almost smell her she was so close. Grandfather nudged me slightly in the ribs, and then gestured toward her, smiling. I tried (and failed, I must admit) to shrug it off. He knew I had some feeling for her and all he wanted was for me to "get on with it," and speak with her--but not here, not now. This was solemn, we were here for another purpose, and my youthful foolishness would (and should) wait.

It wasn't long before we all (much like cattle) were herded off to the burial site. The casket was borne and placed with ropes to the bottom of the freshly dug grave. But this was not the end of the procession. We all formed a circle around and listened--or tried to listen--to the last words of the priest. I was far too busy trying not to notice that Juliana had chosen to stand next to me to hear anything that may have been said.

I knew that if I looked at her, I would be petrified; so I did the only thing I knew: I practically ignored her. A childish and silly thing to do, I know; but I felt almost trapped, and my mind raced for a possible solution. That's what I came up with on the quick. It was, admittedly, not my best effort.

Before I knew it, the rites were complete, and the symbolic handful of soil was cast to the casket. The crowd began to dwindle, and I turned to walk away and that when I felt her hand around my arm.

I froze. Like a deer out in the open. I am sure I was just as wide-eyed as any doe.

"I hate good days like this being ruined," she said. "Will you walk with me?"

These may have been the most words spoken by her to me ever. I doubt I will ever forget them.

The best I could muster was "Of course!"

I am sure I sounded far less intelligent than I will choose to remember later. We walked from the cemetery into a nearby field which bordered on a wood; the trees were green and lush now, dense, deep foliage, green and greedy with life. There was a slight breeze rustling through them. I could hear crickets and bees, and of course her wonderful voice. She spoke of how that death was (from the point of view of the church) not the end, but a beginning; however to her new beginnings could be just as frightening as endings. She liked things to remain as they were, even if there was some good that comes from change.

From there I became more relaxed, I had never thought of her as someone approachable and as casual as myself, I had always seen her as something precious (this is something I only admitted to myself, but I know Grandfather knew.) I wonder if he had planned this timely meeting and walk, I turned to look back but did not see him--surely he had gone home--along with the rest of the sorrowful mourners.

Juliana had stopped, and dropped her hand from my arm. I turned back to her, and there we were, she and I, a scant few yards from it.

There in the woods, hidden in the dark shade, was a wolf-form. Large, bristling, low-growling and looking at us with teeth bore. One could just barely see its outline in the shade. Highlighting the form was the eyes, which were like candle-lights reflected in a mirror. It was dark as night there in the wood, and mid-day here in the field; two worlds apart, separated by only feet.

Staring at the wolf, I cannot tell you how scared we were, because, honestly, I don't know how to judge such a thing. We stared at it, and it stared back. Juliana was practically immobilized in terror. If it were possible to communicate when one locks eyes, we certainly would have words, the wolf and I. I do not know what I would learn from the mind of such an animal, but I am certain it would learn quite a lot from me.

It snarled, growled, and clearly wanted to harm us; however, curiously, it would not (or perhaps could not) step out into the light. It tried, probing with a paw, it's eyes never leaving ours, it would touch down gingerly--more daintily than I would have imagined a beast so powerful and large would be able--only to pull back again. There was no wince of pain, no indication of issue at all: simply that it would not enter the light from the sun, preferring to remain obfuscated in the very dense foliage of the woods. Perhaps it thought this a trap, cunningly set for it by myself and Juliana.

I--slowly--took Juliana's hand. It was cold. The blood had left her extremities; and there was sweat running down her neck. She breathed rapidly, her eyes never leaving the beast. I pulled her arm toward me. She didn't move, but her arm did. It was as if she had been rooted--nailed firmly--to the ground. Her feet never quavered and she made no noise except for her hurried breathing. As I touched her the beast growled deeply again, indicating its extreme displeasure with the situation.

Again I quickly turned to see if there was anyone remaining near the grave-side, but all had left leaving only Juliana and I in the field. I returned my gaze to the animal--now was definitely the time I wished I could communicate with it, but I saw nothing in its eyes but malice. With an intractable foe, one is usually left with the option to flee when fighting is a losing proposition; but I did have one possibility for victory.

I readied a memorized enchantment, the same one, in fact, that I had used before (albeit without much accuracy)--the bolt of fire. Knowing that most animals fear fire and will recoil from it instinctively. They know the devastation flame can cause, and I would use that knowledge to my advantage should the need arise; but I didn't want to loose such power. Juliana would react, I think, most unexpectedly should she know what capability I might have in the area of what most would call occult, and should she come to the conclusion that it would be better if I were reported to the local priests, sure as the sun rises each morning I would be held as apostate and heretic; and the punishment would be most severe.

So, I did the next best thing. I readied a plan for escape. I pulled her toward me in a jerk. She stumbled, and I caught her. The beast wanted to lunge at us, that was obvious, but it didn't flinch, it was too wary of the invisible line that separated the dark from the light.

"Come, Juliana..." I said, and forced her to turn from the woods (and the wolf) and in a seeming daze with a gait that shown her true state of fear.

We walked away, all the while the wolf stayed where it was in the dark, in the wood, angry but impotent against our departure. I turned once to look back at it (out of my own paranoia that it was going to charge none-the-less) only to see it but briefly, before it turned and headed back into the dark trees with movement and speed that only truly wild animals possess.

As we walked, she caught her breath again, and choked a bit and covered her mouth. She had a well of tears borne by stress and fear in her eyes.

"...It..." she stammered, "It was going to kill us!"

"It's over now," I comforted, holding her tighter about the waist. "Let's return you home."

She didn't say anything, just nodded in agreement. Try as she might to hold her resolve, she could not: some fears are too powerful to deny and once felt take a deep hold. Tears cascaded down her cheeks like a waterfall. She stopped walking, and began blubbering, crying, shaking as I held her in my arms.

For the brief moment I held her, I wished to be lost in that instant for eternity. I closed my eyes and smelled her hair, felt her warmth, and could sense her heart beat return to normal. In that instant I was transported again, a daydream, in a return to how I always pictured her in my sleep: crowned and wearing finery, her hair as a fiery halo, smiling. I held her and was truly happy in that delusion.

But all too brief are the seasons of womanhood, and change like the winds they will; for it is the wont of men to believe that women need us as protector, friend, lover, and wall; but the truth is far more complicated than the reason of men can contain.

She pulled from me, my daydream faded as I snapped back to the world as-it-is, and she straightened herself, wiping the tears from her face.

In an uncomfortable silence I escorted her home, all the while wishing with all that there might be within me to hold her once again.

On the return trip home, and all that night, all I could think of was that I should have kissed her. The opportunity was made complete by the semi-heroics I had performed: I saved her from the animal; surely a kiss would have been a welcome form of payment?

Bah! I tossed and turned in my bed, unable to fathom my clumsiness and folly. I had the greatest chance a man had ever been granted, and I had completely and utterly foiled it; and I was certain that the like would not come again.

I could not sleep. I needed a diversion from this madness--I should have stayed with my studies in sorcery than to have half-embroiled myself in the amour of a woman. But then, my mind brought me solace from the tumult and storms of emotion: the book.

Beneath where I lie, the pages called forth to me. Surely, this would ease me at least somewhat. I reached into the straw and pulled out the pages. Opening it randomly, I found a page that piqued my curiosity. I hadn't seen it before when rearranging the pages when they had earlier come loose from the binding. Here before me was a treatise, written in scratched writing, about those things that rise from the dead on the third day with an insatiable lust for blood and immortality:

vampires.

Of course, I had heard the word before. I always considered them a folk-tale and nothing more. After all, I had never seen, nor heard of, such a thing actually existing; and Grandfather never mentioned them either, nor any of my mentors, such as the late Doctor--they couldn't actually exist, I concerned myself. It must be impossible.

But my mind, in the candle-light, plowed through this sense with a single thought: why shouldn't they exist when sorcery--the very art I practice daily--exists as well when there is no earthly reason that it should?

Call it sleep-induced lunacy, but I was willing to believe that if the energy I can call into being is real, and were considered tales by others, why then should not the tales I considered false be, in fact, true? Therefore, I reasoned, vampires exist; or perhaps they did exist, and are no longer among us (which I hoped.) It is quite two different things to say "Here is a thing," and "There once was a thing." I took comfort in that thought, that these undead that feed on the living might not actually be, and I read on.

I devoured the whole chapter about them--their ways (of which there was not much)--their weaknesses, which confounded me supremely. I had been taught that vampires could not walk out in the sun for it would burn them to dust, but this is apparently untrue. They can--or as I had prayed, perhaps did but do so no longer--walk in the sun, like any of us would, but were made profoundly weak by it. Their forms would be frozen and they could not alter their shape, as the most powerful are known to do, and their other abilities were very low: the youngest of them might not have access to use inhuman capabilities at all. They were most vulnerable in the day, which is why they customarily chose to rest when the sun was high; however, they were still powerful foes with the strength of many men.

How they lived--and I use that word very loosely--was interesting to me: they used a form of mesmerism to dull the senses and cloud the minds of those upon whom they wished to feed. There would be no screaming, no thrashing of arms, no wailing or running away. Simply a succumbing to the power of the ancient mind that was probing them, a wanting to be fed upon would be engendered, and once allowed, they could take from the victim whatever nourishment needed, leaving the dead or severely anemic person to the elements.

Not every vampire kills their prey, I learned: many of them feed only lightly, taking little and not harming greatly, and leaving a subconscious thought of something else in the mind--it would be as if the attack had never happened. In this way, the vampire could return nightly, or at least more frequently, to draw blood (and life) from the populace of men--not unlike how a farmer milks a cow and the cow is not harmed. Whereas we feed on lower forms, we are ourselves fed upon by a superior predator.

And immortality would be their prize.

I was enthralled by the idea of such potency, power, and the concept of living forever. I could feed on persons, without killing, I assured myself. Death would never come to my door, and I would have forever to research my skills: it wouldn't matter if *Dies Irae* came for me with hot brands and desire for my blood, I would simply take their vital fluid instead!

I would have read more, but I thought I heard a stirring from Grandfather, and quickly put the pages from where I had taken them. It was nearly daylight now, and I still had not slept; but it didn't matter, I was exhilarated and embraced of new knowledge and had found a new thing to research in secret: What would it take to become a vampire and were there any at all? Having read about them my familiarity grew and I was not afraid.

That morning, while preparing our meal, I informed Grandfather about the strange wolf activity after the funeral, something he was keen on only slightly; he didn't seem to consider it all that out of place for a wild animal to refuse to come from its point of ambush into the open. Though I thought it odd, he simply passed it off as a skittish animal acting, perhaps, to protect its young.

"Difficult to say, really," He mentioned, "But luckily you had your wits about you to protect Juliana," and of that, nothing more was said.

With having prepared our morning meal, I took the opportunity to ask Grandfather--in a sly manner--about my latest interest in vampires.

"Grandfather?" I quipped while sipping, "Something occurred to me, and I wanted to ask you about it..."

"Oh?" Came is simple reply.

"Yes, I was thinking: if our art exists, and it is considered to be faerie tales by others, would it be possible that things we consider mere tales might actually be true?"

He drank some and thought a bit, not showing any real

concern, indicating that he thought this mere idle breakfast banter.

"Yes, I'd suppose it would," he answered in time.

"Really?" I answered in turn, "Do you think so? My reason for asking was--well, because of the wolf encounter," --and here I was fibbing a bit, but wanted to pass it off as true-- "It made me think about some of the more despicable tales I've read about..."

"Such as?" He was still not concerned and began to drain his cup.

"Well," I stammered, "Vampires, for one."

I admit, this was heavy-handed as far as bringing up a delicate subject goes; but there was no easy way I could say it. I worried he might think I was on to something, but he was made flustered more so than anything, I feel. At any rate, he showed no particular concern in that direction. I could tell this because at that moment he gulped hard and nearly choked on the broth. Sputtering and spilling on his tunic and lap he winced a bit.

"Good Lord! What made you think about those things?"

I answered his question with one of my own in a near interrupting, excited manner.

"Do you think they exist?"

I wanted to divert his questioning from me as I was uncomfortable with prolonging any form of deception; he was someone whom I loved dearly, and I would not choose to harm him further.

"Well..." He stumbled, "I suppose, yes, uh..."

An uncomfortable pause was quickly covered with "I think perhaps that the very idea..."

He was searching for some answer that I felt he didn't actually have or didn't know how to approach and would have revealed more were it not for the knock that came at the door, which was immediately greeted by Grandfather exclaiming "Oh, thank heavens!"

Quickly he popped up and went to answer it himself. Usually, it was my duty to answer the door; it was clear he wanted out of the particular line of questioning and took the path of least resistance--a visitor. Whatever the answer he might have been planning to offer didn't matter to me; and I smiled a little smirk knowing that he had been caught off-guard and that, whatever mastery he had in matters of sorcery, there would be no more information of real value on the topic at hand.

I smiled more when I saw who it was our morning visitor was, Juliana. Standing tall, and dressed well, looking like a sparkling stone in shallow clear water, hair gently blowing in the cool morning breeze.

"Locarno, I believe she's here for you. Either that, or I am a very lucky man."

"Yes, Locarno, sir," she said, softly, almost blushing.

I rose to greet her and nearly fell from my stool. I caught myself and didn't plant my face into the floor, which I considered fortuitous, as I would appreciate not embarrassing myself so early in the morning.

I met Grandfather's gaze then, he had a twinkle in his eye and a smile across his lips. I knew then that my day's chores had just come to an end; and that, whatever might follow, he was excited to see that it appeared Juliana was as interested in me as I was in her, as was obvious to him; and there was no reason to hide this fact further.

"Juliana!" It might have sounded more excited than I had planned, but since I doubted I'd see her again so soon, I think I could be forgiven the slight exclamation.

I met her eyes with mine, and reflexively inhaled--it was as if she was the very source of fresh air, and I felt quite strengthened by it.

She reached out her arm, and took my hand, "Come, walk with me, please."

I turned nearly stone-faced and shocked to Grandfather, who motioned outside with his hand; and just like that, with a slight coy laugh, she pulled me into the bright morning sun.

I walked out into the bright morning, blinking and unfocused; yet I could not take my eyes of Juliana. As always, she was radiant. Nearly as soon as I was through the archway, Grandfather closed the door behind me--a subtle nudge into manhood, I suppose; or perhaps he didn't want to intrude on our privacy. Either way, there I was with her.

She took my hand gently, and we walked out into the field toward the birch trees and the stream. Slowly, she took my arm and placed it around her neck and placed hers around my waist. (Still walking as though I was in a bit of a shock.) Always she was so proper, this seemed to me to be out of character or place. Not that I minded it at all.

"Today, because of your gallantry, I have prepared a lunch for us and a day by the stream. Father always said that good men are to be rewarded for their efforts."

Were I a man of greater power, I would have frozen time at that very moment. The wind in her hair was fragrant, the field was filled with buzzing life, the sun in the sky was warm and inviting, and on my arm was a woman of great poise and even greater beauty whose company I enjoyed immensely.

We approached a spot overlooking the water where a large sheet lay and a basket nearby with lids closed and a bottle protruding. She has had quite some time to prepare before she came to my door. This was all very well thought out. The spot was well chosen. The water was close enough to hear it, but not so close as to be loud and interrupting. The grasses were shorter allowing us to recline or sit with ease, and it was a bit secluded so we wouldn't be bothered. Juliana had thought of everything.

This day, I knew, was to be something special. I said a silent prayer: let the hours be like days; let us be.

We spent the day talking, laughing, eating and wandering the light woodland bordering the stream. I learned much about her then. For instance, I learned that she loved the smell of freshly cut long grasses, and that if she could be any animal in the world it would be a butterfly.

On that, I had to know "Why?"

The simple answer was perfect.

"They're colorful, light, harm none, and are pleasant to look at--and what's more, they fly!"

"But why not a bird? They fly as well," I replied.

"Birds are nasty, loud creatures; and besides, they soil statues. I like statues."

It seemed so well planned; I had no choice but to agree, even if I didn't understand how or why she came to these decisions. I knew then she was more thoughtful than I and she was filled with wonder at the natural world. Were I to have a thousand years with her in my wished-for frozen-time I would only be able to delve just so deep. I do not believe I could learn everything to know about her, women should always be a mystery to men. This is the way things ought to be. Perhaps, this is what it meant to be a woman: to have infinite time to dwell on things; whereas a man is busy with war and commerce, the woman, innately or reflexively, understands and dwells upon other, more serene, things.

From her basket, she pulled something quite exquisite--something wonderful: grapes. I hadn't had grapes since last year, how she managed to get them I do not know, but her family does have influence, so she must have used it to obtain them and I should simply revel in the luxury that was offered before me.

I sat on the soft linen she had prepared and she sat before me, reclined into me, and I held her then and stared off into the fields across the stream. Her scent mingled with that of the wild flowers that surrounded us. I closed my eyes, and as transported to my dream-world. She relaxed against me, and in my mind's-eye I saw her as that which I always did--crowned as a queen, adorned in mink and sable, with children at her feet, and a wonderful smile on her lips, gazing at me through the strange, undefined window.

Opening my eyes I saw that in this reality she was still there, eating grapes while feeding some to me, dwelling in my arms with her own eyes shut. I think now, in this place, I understand what the priests had always been trying to explain heaven felt like--or perhaps the old myths of the Elysian Fields--I didn't care which. All I knew is that this day, were it to stretch on forever, which would be just fine with me.

I never expected this. Always had I been so focused on my craft, my work, my art. I didn't examine at all the possibility that a woman would enter my life and bring with it such abject joy. When I look down on her face, and when she smiles up at me in return, I know things in my heart that make no sense in the world. Is this what love is? I think so, and it is glorious.

Neither the brave nor bold are either of those unless they are men of action, conviction, and courage. The ancient stories tell us that to win the battle, the day, or the heart one must make a leap of faith. One must trust in the gods, or in one's self. But to know these things is one matter, and it is quite another entirely to be those things. How does one truly muster the inner fortitude and strength to admit to others (or perhaps themselves) the things that must be, or are, true?

Would I be so stupid, so blind, as to miss the opportunity? Would my fears and folly follow me, hound me, sedate me into inaction? Or would I, as a person with a beating heart and emotion have the wherewithal to do (or to say) the things that boil within--and would the consequences be more than could be borne by a single soul?

Had I--in this brief moment--gone utterly mad?

No. I had instead recognized that which had been before me the whole time. As I looked at her, and she at me, I must have made an odd contortion of my face, for she looked with slight befuddlement and asked the question--the most difficult of questions--that can ever be turned toward a man in my condition. "What are you thinking about?"

With it there, in the open, in the wind, for all to hear, it became a moment of reality. The question was spoken and (as they say) come Hell or high-waters I must answer. But how? I could be nonchalant about it, or I could do the thing that scares men and drains one of their vigor into inaction?

On this day, and for the thousand days yet to come, I would ponder the reason why, but in that instant the voice of my father came forth from within me--one of his greatest lessons: speak the truth in love.

"Juliana," I paused. "I... love you."

With that, she nearly leapt up to her knees, turned to me face to face, nose to nose, and with deep breath taken she interwove her fingers in mine, leaned forward and kissed me in a way that would make angels swoon and the devil blush. The word that can only be used is passionate. She dove deep into the water that was my soul.

On that day, I was bold; and with her I would know no fear, forever.

Boldness, as you know, can take many forms: from the head-long rush into battle, to the broad strokes of a painter with a sure hand. There are just as many definitions of bold acts as there are people that perform them. With Juliana, my boldness would, to some, be considered an outright mistake--one to be lamented much in later days--but I, honestly, could not care what others thought at this moment in time. With my being inter-twined with her in that field, our clothing all astray, it was like a brief glimpse of heaven above.

A woman's body is a mystery. Whereas a man is rough, square, flat, and broad; a woman is quite the opposite--smooth, soft, round, warm--and in every possible way more natural than that of a man. Juliana has these curves of young womanhood; she is defined by soft flesh and subtle sways. Because of this, I began to understand with great clarity the writings of Sappho, which before seemed filled with emotion unfathomable to me.

Were a man to try, and even more so, were he even possessed of the power to do so, he could not create anything as absolutely genuine as a woman. This is not to say that men haven't tried. I knew from the to-date albeit short foray into the forbidden book that there were necromancers who wished to take parts of other beings, graft them together, and create a composite creature, living and animate. But the perfection of a collection of parts is always in doubt when the final form is unnatural. To even think opposite of such would be madness.

The closest any man had ever come to making something so wonderful as a woman were the master sculptors chipping away at marble and hewn rock; and even then, with all their skill, they cannot make a living being, endowed with that spark of life that denotes them as a living thing, sentient, intelligent, emotional, and altogether human. They can only imitate in rude, crude form that which already exists. Mere copies of the grandeur that is existent in the world.

Juliana has that spark of life, but in her it is more like a blazing inferno. She revels in life, the living, in people, and for some reason, in me. That spark, that smile, that laugh--were I able, I would curl up within it and live (if only such were tangible things that from which such a tapestry could be woven.) She was my absolute focus, I knew this; and I wasn't wrong to figuratively take my heart out and show it to her. I had been, in fact, rewarded with far more than I gave. This woman, here in my arms, is more valuable than the sun, the moon, the stars, and even her beloved butterflies.

I wanted nothing more than to feel her warmth around me, and this attraction was returned from her somehow magnified as if by a great lens. But we dare not be found in this state, lest we face consequences that we would rather not dwell upon. If one wants to be literal, what we were doing was adultery and fornication--and emotion and love notwithstanding--the penalties could be quite severe, so we (sadly) were a bit quick in our coupling.

To say that my--or rather, our--first foray into lovemaking was hurried, unkempt, and probably very unromantic would be (at the very least) true. It was wild, reckless, silly, awkward, and a bit painful for us both--grasses, reeds, and sticks are not something to be reclined upon for anything requiring such a delicate state.

I cringe to even mention the fist-sized rock that nearly split my head open. Luckily for me, only a little pain would remain long-term; but at the moment, in the heights of it all, a sharp jab to the base of the skull was not what for which I had a longing.

As we clothed ourselves, hurriedly, I grabbed the rock, which I had tossed lightly to the side, and threw it toward the river without looking. I expected to hear a knock of it upon a tree, or perhaps--if my throw was strong--a simple slash into the rushing water.

What I and Juliana heard, however, was something completely different. So different it was, it grabbed our attention, even though we were only half dressed. The sound could only be described as eerily similar to what a large spoon sounds like when you slap an uncooked roast or ham. It was conjoined with a slight crack, and then a moment later a very dull thud.

We stopped immediately, wide eyed, looking at each other. Her bright and passionate smile instantly faded as she gave me a stare that would be easily translated by anyone who saw it; we both wondered it, but only she dared speak.

"What did you do?"

Clearly, she knew. She saw that I had thrown the stone--not violently, not maliciously, only but a toss toward the water--but the question, though she knew what it was I had done, wasn't about what I had done, but rather what was it that had just happened: what change in the local environment had I just discovered (or inflicted)?

The remainder of our clothing went on quickly, and we went off toward the river together to see where my wayward stone may have come to rest. It didn't take long to see what I hit, where it was, and to hear the screams Juliana made when she saw her very first corpse.

With all the events that had happened--namely the Doctor's death and my budding relationship with Juliana--I had forgotten that I had not seen Madame Beck in some time. She had not been present for her morning meeting with Grandfather--and now I knew why.

Once Juliana's scream died out, she turned into me and I held her tight, her face was buried into my chest as I tried to comfort her; all the while I was not taking my eyes off of the Madame's now semi-bloated and cyanic body as it lay there in the shallow stream. An argument could be made that there had been a struggle: her clothing was torn a bit, very out of place (especially for her), and a shoe had floated away from her a short distance, and there was some dried blood near her mouth--also her eyes were fixed, glazed, in horror at some sight which was certainly the last she saw.

Though I stood there only moments, it seemed like an eternity. Juliana was crying almost out of control, and the streams down her cheek began to dampen my shirt. I had once been told that the tears of a woman borne out of love or compassion are holy and those that witness them are blessed. These tears were from fear, the waters were cold and I was not blessed by the presence. I would have given my arm to turn their tide. But though I have some semblance of power I am but a man, and some things that are done are impossible to undo.

I scanned Madam's body from our distance, to learn what I may. And so I saw, and then knew, that this was no accident--for there, darkened by her time in the water, was the unmistakable mark which I had only became aware of quite recently but knew all too well: a half obscured sun with five emanating rays.

Dies Irae had brought death again. Whomever they are, they had become bolder, the mark was not hidden from view as it was on the good Doctor; rather it was there, in plain sight--emblazoned near perfect center on her upper chest just below her chin.

How she was strewn was no mistake, no happenstance, no accident. She did not float here from upstream--that would have been impossible, her girth (which she carried with ease in life) would have made her too liable to strike the creek-bed and hang her stuck and immobile. Her arms were placed almost gently into the sand; her head straight and proper. She had been posed in that particular manner for a reason--one I surmised was so that she might purposefully be found, identified, and the mark upon her be seen as prominent. This was a message, although the meaning may be unclear.

Within seconds, Grandfather and two other neighbors arrived from across the fields.

One said "What the..." and it trailed off, not wishing to complete the utterance.

Grandfather whispered to me to take Juliana back to our home. I nodded, we turned, and we went. I stopped only briefly to pick up her basket--the one she brought for our day in the sun--the blanket would be left. Grandfather had picked it up and used it to cover Madame's body. As we walked slowly home the murmurs of their voices faded behind us. The morning, so filled with promise, now turned dismal even in the bright unobstructed and cloudless day.

Back home, Juliana was still in shock. I took her to my bed, and placed her there to rest. It was difficult to pull her arms from my tunic, she had a grip on them that defied logic: her hands were lithe, and one would never expect that she would be possessed of such might.

As I lay her down I told her to rest. She nodded. I went to turn to place the basket on the table, and she reached out to me, and with that great unbelievable strength grabbed my hand. It was clear, I would not be leaving her side for quite some time.

She trembled, but at least the tears had stopped. It took her only moments to fall into slumber. Being who she is, she was not one to become accustomed to seeing death so close--for that matter, neither was I--but I had the unfortunate luxury (if I might malign an otherwise good word for this purpose)--of having seen the Doctor in a similar condition; that is to say, in a state of no longer being counted as one of the living.

I set the basket down, careful to not have the expensive crystal within jostle and thereby awaken her. She needed rest, and I was determined to give it to her as best I could. She'd been through a lot in such a short period of time--from our coupling to seeing a decomposing person. I cannot imagine what thoughts, what possible nightmares, this day might engender.

Leaving the room slowly, I closed the door, not fully, but enough that she had a semblance of privacy to which a young woman might be accustomed should she rise. I stepped outside for a moment to clear my head. I closed my eyes and stood still. The sun was warm, the wind blew, the sky was clear, and as I breathed the fragrance of distant flowers was present. All this could not clear my senses fully. I knew we were all in grave danger; *Dies Irae* would not stop voluntarily until they had accomplished their goal. What their goal might be, I was not certain.

I opened my eyes, and saw Grandfather approach, and with him was Juliana's brother. Both made haste toward me.

"Where is she?" Simm, the Younger, requested.

"Inside. She's sleeping," I replied.

"I will get her and take her home."

"No," came Grandfather, "Let her be. She's had enough for today--or for any number of days. She is safe here."

Simm would have, I could tell, argued the point and entered to take her but we were spared of this by another calling him from down by the stream--requesting he bring his cart and horse. He nodded in relative agreement and strode off to obtain what was requested. No doubt it would be used to carry Madame's body away from the river. I was grateful for the lack of a confrontation on the matter.

I turned to Grandfather, "*Dies Irae* again. I saw the marking."

"So did I." He trailed. "This we must not reveal to any. Should others learn of *Dies Irae*, things could become much worse."

What he meant by that, I didn't know; but I knew that I didn't want things worse than they had become, so I agreed without hesitation.

He placed his hand on my shoulder in supportive manner, "Locarno, look after the girl, I will return when I am able." Just then he was called for by name, and he turned and walked toward the waters from which we had all just come. I saw the militia-men approach in the distance, murder will draw them and I only hoped they didn't make things worse--if that was indeed possible.

I turned and re-entered our home, stepping in and closing the door behind me, my eyes adjusted to the lower light level, I saw Juliana standing there, in the archway to my room holding in her hands the contents of the black tome.

"I couldn't rest. I reached for you, but you were gone, when I rolled over this poked me. Why was it in your bedding?"

I am sure that the blood must have drained from my face in an instant. If it hadn't it certainly would have done so when she opened the book and started to read from it. Juliana was educated, and spoke at least one other language, but how much more she might know we were about to find out.

While I stopped and stared at her while she was reading from the book, I could hear her intoning words that I had not yet read from within its ebon binding. I knew it was Italian; and it seems she'd started mid sentence, had skipped ahead, reading from some perhaps random passage contained therein; and as she began to speak the words I prayed to myself that she didn't read anything too damning.

"*...Sulla convocazione della Bestia Di Mano E Gli Occhi, si ricordino della venuta del viaggiatore, che porta la morte a chi convocare con i demoni...*"

Oh, God! I knew what that meant. That was a brief part of a ritual I briefly glanced over before about summoning a powerful entity from beyond this world. I doubted she could have found a more incriminating phrase from which to read.

I was in big trouble. A vision flashed through my head of being burned at the stake, skin flayed from the fire, with the elders of the church and accompanying monks from the local monastery encircling me making the sign of the cross, sprinkling me with holy water--casting out evil and condemning my soul all at the same time. I felt cold, and there was good reason to fear.

There followed a pause. I stood my ground and felt week in the knees. That which I had hidden (I thought so well) was there, in the open before me, held by someone more precious than air, a woman whom I trusted--my folly and doom was there within its binding. She held it in her hands at first casually, but with growing trepidation as she realized what it was that was there on the page, and the implications thereof.

She spoke again, "I...I think this is talking about summoning a demon...or something... There's more here about a man who isn't truly a man, who comes when you attempt, and if you are not swift, he brings '...*Morte, con potenze da oltre...*' --'Death with power from beyond!'"

She stopped reading and looked at me. My eyes were wide and my heart was pumping. I felt a little faint, and might have met the floor had she not spoken to me directly, which forced me to answer.

"Locarno, what is all this?"

At this point I could have generated a lie, or a ruse (if you will), but this woman deserved better than that and any lie I thought up on the spot would have been plainly obvious as she looked at me with her sparkling eyes, still bloodshot from tears. I would have been, in that moment, transparent as glass; and that would have made things infinitely worse.

This day, for her, would be marked as one of the worst ever--having seen death so close. I had hoped before the body of Madame had been found that the day would be recognized as the day that was ultimately better than any day save the day she was wed. For me, the day had began filled with wonder, only turning sour at the end--and turning even worse now that I stood there, clenched, shocked, filled with dread facing she whom I loved and that anathema text. I should have burned that thing when I had the chance, and now I would most definitely pay for my insolence.

I summoned my strength, closed my eyes, took a breath which generated no solace, and--with shaking hands and protruding heart-- spoke out loud about my art, my craft, my doom.

"It is a book of sorcery--spells and rituals."

My words filled the air, almost echoing. They hung there like birds of the sea riding the air and seemingly motionless in the sky.

I opened my eyes, expecting her gaze to destroy me (or worse, if that would be imaginable), or for her to make cries of blasphemy and to call aloud for her brother--or the militia--who we both could hear, although distant, but were certainly within the range of hearing any cries she might make.

Her eyes were wide with the revelation I made; but she then brought them narrow and pierced me with them, like lightning. It was difficult in that instant to tell if she was ready to point the accusatory finger in my direction, which would cause me to be hauled away as heretic; or if she thought me a simple liar, and that this was all some sort of joke or hoax at her expense.

Her next utterance made her intent clear, what she meant, and what this meant for us both; and it is the second truly great turning point in my relationship with her.

"Show me, please," as she handed me the pages.

She wanted to know, she wanted proof of the claim--crazy as it may sound--that I had just made. Was she handing me just enough rope with which to hang myself? Was I to incriminate myself before her by generating evidence of my crime? It was not too late still to brush this off as some lame attempt at foolery; I could still obtain the book and toss it into the fire, after all.

Or, I could do something righteous and forthright.

I stumbled over the next few words, and in all honesty I do

not to this very day remember them completely; but I knew I acquiesced and gingerly took the collection from her hands, then told her that, as with all great stories or works, it is best to start at the beginning, and to begin very small, as all things invariably do. We retreated back into my room from whence she rose early from her slumber, closing the door behind me (for privacy), she sat on the bedding and I began to extol that which others would claim virtue-less.

And it was there, in the side room sitting on my bed of straw I began to tell Juliana of what sorcery was, what it could accomplish, and how I learned of it. I could tell that she was not moved by the tale, even though it took more than an hour.

"You must be mad, or joking with me."

"None of the like," I expressed.

In order drive home the very point I was trying to make, I showed her something unnatural, something impossible, something that could only come into being were magic a reality in this banally prosaic world--I created light in the palm of my hand. It cast long shadows on the floor and wall, the light was as bright as the sun, and shadows cast darker than the deepest night.

And when the spell faded, her aspect changed.

"Oh, my!" She said softly, and looked up at me with the same eyes she had when she kissed me earlier that day.

I had inspired awe. I made the right choice. I smiled, and sat next to her. She turned to me and glanced coyly at the gathering of pages on the edge of my bed.

"What else can you do?"

In an inexplicable answer seething with unearned bravado-- and now I know that it is the true doom of men that they should strive to impress a woman, throwing caution and sense to the wind--I whispered playfully, "Anything you want."

But as with all youth, I was foolish and cared not for what tomorrow might bring.

She reached for the leaves, handing them to me, drew closer

and begged "Tell me more!"

In the brief moment that her words echoed in my ears, I thought to myself that if I were to show her something from this book, perhaps it should be something of which there was, at least, some form of detail. It was then, with a hesitant whimper I opened the book to the passages I recently read about--the same passages that I had questioned Grandfather over--the collected knowledge on vampires.

Basically, all I did was read from the book to her, retelling what I already knew: what they were, how they lived, that they drew blood from the living. Nothing special, really. I'm sure being an educated woman she may have surmised much of this material already. After all, vampires appear in popular tales, jokes, and plays.

After reading a passage or two for her, I glanced up at her and could tell that she was unmoved. This wasn't a spell, this was a treatise, and that meant she was bored.

No, hearing me chatter on wasn't what she had in mind when she asked for more; rather she wanted to see something happen, not hear about it. So I turned to a new section while giving her an apology by way of a sheepish grin and without even previewing what was on the page I began to read aloud again.

"Ewige Leben," the German text began as I read, which is to say, 'Eternal Life,' (and I will continue by translating into English), "Could be obtained by various means and potions; and the process to be described herein is but only a sample of the possibilities."

I darted my eyes up to hers and could see that the words had some power over her. She said the words back to me, in a whisper, for they had clearly gained her attention and sparked her imagination, "Eternal life..."

I had stopped reading at that point, but she goaded me to continue.

"To prepare oneself for the process of immortality takes no effort; it is the accumulation of the materials which takes time. Necromancer, find yourself a phial or crystal decanter of small size--"

"Necromancer?" she interrupted.

She didn't know the word, or she wavered at the use if she did understand it. I attempted to explain.

"Often, that's the word used to refer to a sorcerer, nothing to worry about."

She accepted this, and gestured that I return. She actually wanted to hear the words.

"For it is within this container you shall place your soul, and while it exists you shall live for all time."

The text went on to explain that the container should be made of crystal specifically, and from the highest quality, capable of withstanding demanding use--was not delicate and likely to crack or break as that would be disastrous.

"Well," I said, "It appears there are reagents needed as well."

Continuing, "Blood of self, blood of love, hair of both, spider's silk shall stretch thin the thread of life."

Clearly this ritual would take time to accommodate the needs. I looked up at her. That's when I discovered I had been momentarily lost in thought; Juliana had stood and opened the basket from our earlier outing and had pulled from it a blue crystal oil container. We had used the oil that once was in it with our bread. She turned to me holding it in her hands. It was about the size of her fist, and tightly capped with its cork-lined stopper. She had a smile on her face, and then sat next to me again.

"We have the phial," she almost sang the words, "But what does blood of self and blood of love mean?"

"Self is 'you'--or, rather, the person performing the ritual; and the 'blood of love' would be the blood of someone loved--a wife, perhaps."

"Or lover," she chimed in, while touching my arm.

I knew what that meant; I would be expected to perform this spell for her. I had not prepared, I knew only what was read aloud. That is not how one should perform sorcery: preparations are key to success. I took from her the oil glass, and placed it upon my desk, and I told her, simply, that I would need time to prepare.

"Tomorrow, then?" she asked.

I have to admit, the look on her face was exquisite, and her eyes, before which I can only describe myself as transparent, made me answer in the affirmative. She smiled again, leaned forward and hugged me.

My eyes were open, and still I felt myself transported away by her touch. I could see The-Queen-That-She-Is in my mind so clearly. If only those embraces lasted for all time.

But all things end, even grand visions, when called back into reality by an outsider.

"Juliana!" Came the cry from outside. "Let us be home, it is near dark!"

It was her brother, he'd come back for her in order to escort her home. I looked out the window, and sure enough he was correct-- the sun had nearly set. As tradition dictated in our town, she could not remain here once the last rays of light were gone. (An ancient protective belief against possible actions considered unseemly.)

With his return that meant the body of poor dear Madame had

been whisked away to some location, probably preparing for her funeral--which would come sooner than later, considering the condition in which her corpse was when found. Juliana and I rose, I hid the pages quickly under my bedding, and we exited the front of the home just as Grandfather came up beside Simm.

"We must be off," Simm gave as greeting.

"Indeed, I did not know the time," was her stern reply.

She turned to me as if to grant a farewell, but Grandfather spoke just as her lips parted to speak.

"Locarno, assist Simm. Escort Juliana home."

Grandfather probably would have taken the trip himself, but I could tell he was troubled and tired. It had been a long day for us all. Before we set foot to the path, Simm looked at Juliana, and then to me. Seeing that his sister was in good shape and not appearing in any way distraught, he returned his gaze to mine, and his mood seemed to soften. I think in that instant he was grateful, but the abruptness of our departure then made it difficult to know for certain.

And so it was: There we were, mere moments from the doorway being opened and I was in a small walking troupe with her brother in the lead holding aloft a lantern, with Juliana by my side, in a procession in full-view returning to their rather expansive estate; it would take perhaps an hour to walk there and back again. My return would be in the dark, alone.

What is it about the dark of night that freezes the souls of men? Is it that which is contained within; or what might be within? Or is it something more primeval? Are there darker things in the dark night that comes for man? Or is it simply that we cannot see--being creatures of the day with eyes needing light--and we fear that which we cannot know (or more correctly in this case, cannot see?)

I do not know, nor perhaps do I want to know; but I do know that the trek to the estate of Juliana's family was indeed dark. The only light was Simm's lantern, and he was some feet in front of us. For comfort, Juliana was on my arm. I cannot tell if she clung to me for fear of the night; or if it was I who clung to her for the very same reason. Let us then say: we clung to one another, inconspicuously of course.

Periodically, her brother would turn back to see us, making sure, no doubt, that we were still there and that no harm had befallen either--or rather, none had befallen his sister, as I am certain that he really wouldn't bat an eye should I fall off of the face of the world. He loved his family more than anything; or at the very least, more so than he had any concern for me.

We walked not slowly past the deep orchard to our right; and a quicker step propelled us forward. That wood was well known, it had been there for ages, and was on the very perimeter of the land owned by Juliana's family. (Just last year, I saw an apple there as big as my head. I'm told it made a particularly nice pie.) I was, as was everyone, in familiar land. The area in the light of day was open, calm and relaxed; however, in the night all sort of twisted tree limb carved mockery of the boldness of men and made unnerving shadows against the darkest possible blue sky of night.

I thought to myself, if there were things there in the wood, and should they come for us, we would have to possess the speed of wind to make it to the front gate of her home. An ambush here would be most unfortunate indeed.

Even now, I damn myself for having said that though none heard it. For it is as if my worst fear had become manifest. Just then was the time when the howling and growling commenced from that same wood, those same trees, which in the light of day would brook no evil. We were watched, we were known, we were vulnerable; and there in the road, Simm stood, halted, holding aloft his lantern.

He stopped because he heard the noises as well. He knew what that meant: that we were in a spot for which none were prepared. It was just he, the sole man; and I, a boy alone beside a girl, standing against wolves (or worse) that were ready for mischief at our expense.

Our beacon, mere moments ago our bastion of hope and life was now our doom: a light in the night is a flame pointing direction, intent, position, and illumination of the prey. Most assuredly they saw us. But we could not see them, just as it is impossible to look from a lighted room into the darkness, within the globe of light of the lantern it was beyond our ability to see into the wood. We were at a distinct disadvantage.

"Locarno, Juliana...to me!" Simm ordered.

We formed a triangle, all three of our backs to each other. And we circled, struggling to see what there was, and what might have made those growls; but now the growls that had come precipitously closer.

"If I tell you, I want you to run," he whispered. "More than anything, Juliana must be protected!"

I knew that was directed at me, and should it be needed I was expected to sacrifice myself for her. I will not say I am a coward, but I am certainly not the bravest man, and I truly hoped that I would not have it come to that foul end.

Juliana softly cried, "Oh, God! I can't do this!"

She lifted her dress to expose her long calves. I'm actually glad she said it, because I certainly was thinking it as well. If these were wolves, how were we to outrun a four-legged beast?

"Yes you can; yes you will!" Simm was stern, yet strangely hopeful in his reply.

I heard a juggling, a clinking, and a squeak. I turned in time to see Simm open the face of the lantern, and he poured some of the oil onto the ground in a rough half-circle at his feet.

"Ready yourself!"

He drew his short sword with his opposite hand and smashed the lantern to the ground.

"Now! Run!" Was his only command.

The oil burst into flame, sending flames nearly my height into the air, highlighting the figure of something unnatural and nasty wearing the clothing of a man with a red robe draped over its shoulders. Yet it was not a man, it was haggard, hoary, and with a short, upturned nose like a bat, eyes of red that pierced the flesh, and teeth borne like sharp needles. It possessed a maw of disgust that issued a wicked scream as it pulled back from the flames that licked at its face.

I don't know what that was, but I felt its miasma; and the stench was overpowering. I nearly fell from that alone. I couldn't breathe, the air was stolen from my lungs, it stung the eyes like a bitter, acrid salt. It was as if a thousand skunks, rotting flesh, dead fish, and mold had piled into a barrel, died, and mated with its own corpse.

The scream, pierced my ears like daggers, it made my head ache instantly; my vision wavered, and I winced in torment. I could feel in my stomach the sound its eldritch voice made, and it induced nausea--I could taste my own bile as my stomach churned under this bizarre assault.

The putrid culmination of such sight, smell, and sound was more than I could take and I began to feel the contents of my lunch swell and begin the slow, acidic climb up my throat. The blood pooled from my head and I began to feel light headed.

I turned to move away, and saw that Juliana had already outstripped my pace easily. I don't know how it is possible for a woman to run so quickly in a dress of that length, but she did. A fleet foot propelled out of mortal fear surely was the impetus, and her long legs moved with driving power, propelling her in a blur.

I ran, and as I ran to follow her, I heard a roar, but it was not a roar; it was words spoken by that disgusting thing and they inspired a form of terror I did not think possible. My heart nearly stopped and I stumbled.

"We come for you!"

I did not need to know or hear more, and I could not. My mind blanked, and all my thoughts were of one desire alone: make it to the gate! I ran, my lungs bursting, I didn't know if that thing was there behind me, or if I had left it in the circle of flame, with Simm.

Juliana sprinted through the wrought iron fence with power and skill; whereas I crashed like a bull, but it mattered not. I was there, inside with her. We shut the gate, and looked to see if her brother could be found.

We watched as the fire died out; and of Simm there was no sight. The night air was lanced by the trailing screams of a valiant man as he was dragged away into the night unseen by a thing I couldn't rightly explain.

"Did you see it?" I shook and spoke.

Forcibly, I had cleared my throat and could speak; else I think I would have showered the gate with the remnants of the contents of my last meal. Still the horrid scent was in my nostrils, and my head burned and I felt as if my eyes were bleeding.

"See what?" Came her exhausted reply. "I ran, what do you think? I wasn't going to look back!"

"See?" She added, "Look!" Holding up her dress a little more I could see that she had in fact ran right out of her shoes. Which I can only assume means they're still there in the road somewhere.

Were it not for what had just happened, this might be a little humorous. We sort of smiled to one another, but only briefly, as we heard another screech and something flew low over us, and we took that opportunity to race into the home properly.

Just as we opened the door, there stood her father, older now than I remember him but still somewhat virile, with her mother and maid behind him. Their shadows grew long from the fire, and the Lady Simm's long hair still perfectly coifed seemed to almost glow from the light cast by the burning logs.

"Father!" she cried in both relief and surprise, and she hugged him.

Though he held her, and clearly she was precious to him, he had one other concern on his mind, "Where is your brother?"

"I...I don't know!" Her reply came at last.

He ushered us into the foyer, closing tightly the door behind us. I could feel the warmth of his fire from here; it was a sign of life in an otherwise dismal night.

Juliana was escorted to her bed, as it was past such time, by the two females. I watched her go up the heavily carved, ornate wooden stairs, and slowly rise out of view. Between the polished banister and rails I caught glimpses of her one last time. At least I had done that which Simm wanted--protect her until she was home and safe. That is to say, I hoped that now we were safe.

"Locarno, is it?" He knew my name, of course, but was merely being polite.

"Yes, sir. It is."

"Good boy. What happened? Where is my son?"

As we sat, over the next few hours I told him what happened, and what I knew about the last moments of his son. I was not about to bring forth everything I knew that wasn't common knowledge about the recent spate of deaths, and then only if he asked directly. (I fully expected in the morning to find Simm's body somewhere in the orchard.) I told him Simm was brave, he defended us both; and that I would not be sitting here now had his son not been so quick to action on our behalf.

He rocked back into his larger-than-life chair. As he wiped his fingers into his mustache, I could tell he held back tears and the impotent rage borne of a man who has lost his child. He wasn't angry with me. No, that would be absurd. He was angry that he--one of the wealthy, the powerful, the magnificent--could do nothing, nor could he have done anything had he been there personally. He hated the message I bore, but held no animosity toward the messenger. His wet eyes flashed in the fire light.

"We must form a search party immediately!" He bounded. "My son must be found!"

With that he called for his man-servant to come forth.

Purposefully, I had been vague, using terms like *thing*, and *creature*, not because I wanted to hide the truth from him, but because I, myself, didn't actually know what it was that attacked us in the road. I had never, not even in my worst nightmares spawned from illness and fever, beheld such a sight as that entity. Though it was obscured in the night, I knew that it was no wild animal. It spoke, it wore garments as a man would, but it was no human.

How does a person know if someone can be trusted with knowledge? Can a person's innate level of honor be measured with a glance? Is trustworthiness something brought on with status, or is there more to the equation? These things I had to be mindful of, so as to not divulge too much and thereby endanger others; but I chose to trust in him and threw caution to the wind.

"It was not a man that took your son, sir. It was something altogether different but wore the vestiments of humanity."

He puzzled my words for a minute, staring into the fire as it cast long shadows on the walls of his home. "What are you saying, son?"

"It had clothing, a red robe, but that doesn't make it a man. It was...inhuman."

He paused, looking at me, pondering my absolutely terrible choice of words. I expected him to pry from me more detail, but what he asked next did not follow my expectation at all.

"A red robe, you say?"

His interest had been garnered by my words--words which showed nothing of importance in themselves.

I nodded in the affirmative. It was then that his butler arrived, but just as quickly the man arrived he was dismissed with a wave of the hand.

"Tell me, did you see a clasp upon it? Or perhaps a broach?"

What was it he was after? What did he know--or think he knew--and why was the garment and jewelry attractive to him? Clearly, he was on to something. But what, I didn't dare guess.

"I didn't notice, sir."

Even as I think on it, I don't recall seeing anything like that on the creature. Though, it might have been too dark to know for certain, or perhaps the clasp was too small to be seen.

"Hmmm..." came his mumbling reply, as if deep in thought. He pondered my answers heavily.

"Maybe nothing. Or nothing worth noting, but my son owns a red robe. It is in his wardrobe now, upstairs."

"It could be a coincidence," I replied. "After all, it's just a robe."

"Is it? Perhaps..."

It was clear, unless you were a dullard, that he knew something but was not telling. In his own mind and thoughts he pondered deeper things, and perhaps he had shared too much just now.

He paused a moment more, and with a jolt stopped his thoughts.

"In the morning, you will be on your way home. Rest now, here by the fire. I will have blankets brought to you."

Then he rose, walked to the stairs, ascended, and was seen no more that night. I did hear several doors open upstairs, their wood and steel hinge-work echoing through the damp air. But soon all was silent. His maid, Lydia, brought several blankets and laid them on the chair which was to act as my bed for the evening. Then, she too, disappeared into areas of the large home and was gone.

Such was the way my evening would draw to a close: unsuccessfully trying to sleep in a chair by a fire in a house that wasn't my own. All the while, outside the winds began to howl mournfully across the yard, through the fence, down the road, to the place where a man stood, and lost, his final ground.

The morning came early. Very early, indeed. When I was awakened by the maid, the sun was already up past the horizon. I was unceremoniously told that I should leave now; and that, no, I could not see Juliana before I left as she was feeling a bit ill. Her mother was taking care of her directly.

Lydia also made a snide comment at the end just before I left.

"I don't know what you told to the master of the house, but it upset him greatly. He's been tearing apart his son's room for the past few hours!"

As I left, I walked out through the gate, closing it behind me, I looked up to where I thought Juliana's room might be--to the windows. I saw someone, whom it was I couldn't be sure, standing there peering down at me. It might have been Juliana, or it might have been her mother. As I closed the gate, the person stepped away from the window into the room and disappeared.

I turned, and headed down the road. I was chilled still, the cold night air hadn't cleared yet even though the sun was up; there was a light fog in the fields, and I could see my breath.

Down from their massive home, I found the place that Simm

protected us from the abysmal creature. The remains of his lantern were there, smashed, in a pile. To the side, I found Juliana's shoes, which I picked up--thinking I could return them at some point. His sword was there as well, dropped no doubt in our hour of need, blade snapped in twain. I didn't feel right in taking it: it was his, and I still held out some obscure hope that he may return to claim it, and one shouldn't touch the sword of a man unrequested.

I looked around, but I saw no real sign of struggle. No blood. I would have thought that, since he was dragged away, there would have been some sign other than the broken lantern, perhaps drag-marks from his boots, or a spray of blood, or torn clothing...anything. But of that sort of evidence to show that some fight had happened at all--there was nothing. I knew this didn't feel right.

Looking to the orchard, it was now lit in the full light of day, and I saw nothing amiss. There were just trees, which the night before were so menacing, from which the creature came--the mere memory of it still chilled me--but the trees didn't show signs of passage of such a thing. They were but trees again and they held no monstrosities in their branches.

What happened here? What really happened, I might never know. Is it cowardly to run when commanded? Is bravery in actuality disobedience? Perhaps I was a coward after all, to not stay and fight. Juliana had been safe; perhaps I could have saved Simm as well. This thought was nonsense, if Simm was no match, then neither was I; and the crime it committed would be doubly heinous.

Continuing on, down the path back to my home, the fog was slowly being burned away by the all powerful rays of the sun. A nice breeze began to flow, and I heard chirping of birds. Next I saw people milling about doing their daily routines. As I walked by, I heard a few remark that they had heard the screams, but were too afraid to find out what was going on. One said that he had learned from a friend that Simm had been killed and that the father was so filled with remorse he couldn't stand to hear his son's name. This was followed by "The poor man!" I think they truly pitied his loss.

There were quite a few awkward glances from people as I passed, it was possible they knew I was involved somehow in the events of the previous night. Or perhaps I simply looked bad. Sleep was not very forthcoming in that chair, and once the logs burned out it became quite cold in the mansion. I felt aches in my bones almost as if mild frost flowed in my veins.

Finally making it home, I open the door to find Grandfather already awake and stirring about in the kitchen. He looked at me with a sharp glance.

"Oh, thank heavens!" I must have startled him.

"Grandfather..." I began and let trail. How does one approach a subject like this? How can I say with the proper dignity that a friend is dead?

"Simm was taken last night. Something grabbed him. I saw it. He's dead."

I have to admit, saying those words was almost painful. I may have not truly liked Simm, but I didn't wish him harm. Grandfather stopped immediately, his eyes wide.

"And Juliana?" His concern for her was palpable; he valued her nearly as much as I.

She, of course, was fine home resting but ill. I informed him of what I knew--the red robe--the teeth, the unearthly stench. He probed for some description of the beast, which I filled in as much as I could--I know I focused more on the stench, the teeth, and my stomach's reaction. I tried, I think, in vain to explain the visceral reaction I had just being in the presence of the thing. Even those many hours later, I could still smell it and taste something hideous--no doubt churned up from my gut.

"Did it touch you?" Grandfather asked while peering me over. "Were you harmed?"

He drew closer and checked my tunic, my arms, my neck and head. He seemed genuinely concerned that I might have come into physical contact with whatever that thing was.

"No," I gave back, "Simm defended us from it. The thing spoke in a growl like I'd never encountered and we ran."

This puzzled Grandfather. "Spoke? What do you mean, it spoke?"

"It said, 'We come for you!'"

Chills went down my arms when I repeated it. I hope I never encountered such again in my lifetime.

He puzzled very briefly at this, then sat with a resigned slump in his chair, "Oh..."

Visibly, he was fine, but his demeanor was shaken. The news I brought was unfortunate, indeed. That's when I heard him lowly speak a word that which I had never known.

"*Necuratul...*"

The very word had the sound of importance, it sounded almost regal, like a title.

"I was wrong, Locarno."

This was a rare admission of guilt more than anything. Sure, Grandfather made mistakes, but for him to say it like this--in that way, with those words--surely this was not good, what would follow next, I could feel it.

I was right.

"The thing you encountered, was what in the old country-- where our family originally was from--was called a *necuratul*. A devil, or more precisely for our purposes, it was one of the things you questioned me about before, a vampire."

"What?" My retort was worthless, but it came out.

He knew I heard; only I was filled with disbelief.

"No, everyone knows vampires are like men, not beast. This-- thing--was far too inhuman to be a vampire!"

That's when I was given information that was not in the treatise I had read, and I wondered how he knew it. This might explain why he was so visibly upset at my earlier question about them.

Vampires during the day take the appearance of men--who they were in the life before turning to what they would inevitably become--but as the night progresses onward they become more feral and wild, possessing ever greater abilities (and thirst) until the sun rises. One can tell a vampire by their features. They are more rugged, wild, with entirely bat-like noses that give a sense of smell unrivaled by any natural creature.

It is with this tool (primarily) they hunt for blood. They take the semblance and clothing of men because they are still men, but they are not man any longer (understandably so.) Their stench, that which nearly floored me, stung the eyes, and stole the air, hurt the head, and created retching was the hallmark of a vampire. It is with this they stun their prey. Once that putrid essence had taken root in the victim, they move in for the kill. I was entirely fortunate to escape.

"Vampires are not what I thought."

I had been led to believe that they were dignified and almost noble; but the popular view is often the incorrect one, and it is with this as well. They were, in reality, things of death, decay, and disgust. They are not to be envied, emulated, or admired.

"No, my boy, they certainly are not. And now, it seems, we have one in our very midst."

There was a learned pause as the information sunk in. Then he spoke once more.

"Who else knows of this?"

"Just the elder Simm, I had to tell him what happened to his son. But he acted so oddly, concerned more about the garment it wore than the death of his kin."

The strange conversation I had with him would still weigh heavily upon me for a while.

"What possible difference could that make, clothing?"

"Circles, Locarno. He moves in different circles than we, and draws upon resources and knowledge we do not; and he is a hard man. I do not believe he has it within him to actually know pain of loss. But you are right, he does seem to know something, or thinks he knows. Regardless, he has a piece of the puzzle we do not, and therefore possesses a clearer picture of the whole."

I found that deeply troubling. My mood darkened as my realization that things had gotten considerably worse for the comprehension I had; and that *normal* was a figment relegated to history.

The realization of what it was that we faced was staring back at us; we could not avoid this terrible confrontation. A vampire was here and we had to deal with it. It had taken Simm, and sure as the sun stood in the sky, this would only get worse. Not to mention we still have the unsolved despicable *Dies Irae* murderers. I secretly hoped that Grandfather was correct in his assertion that *Dies Irae* comes to strike, invoke fear, then leave swiftly (due primarily to their lack of real numbers.) Then at least we would only have this undead with which to treat.

This could not have come at a less opportune time, if there ever would be a time in which murder and the living-dead are acceptable--twin conjoined calamities intertwined with our fate.

I was blunt, "How do we kill it?"

I asked the important question, no fancy turn of phrases to hide my intent.

"You cannot be serious! We haven't the power to defeat undead!"

He huffed as if the very thought was as outrageous as a man strapping on wings and flying to the moon. Undead, even at their most weak, such as during the height of day, are still far stronger than any living man can be. He might as well simply call me mad, the result was the same. Surely, he intended not to offend, but it stung--it was not often I had heard such from him; but then he paused, and with eyes that sparkled an apology he meeked out, "Do you think we could?"

I stared back at him. I wasn't upset. I cannot be, not with him; he was the greatest portion of my family, and to me was more valuable than my pride. He knew by my look I was not angered.

He smiled a little, knowing this was true. But that is not what Grandfather was talking about. He was quick witted, and his opinions were known to change feverishly. Not out of lack of thought, but rather the opposite--he could think around a problem with great dexterity, and from one view he would occasionally change to another; but I hadn't caught his intent because I was on to my next utterance.

"What do we do? Do we inform the church?"

When your enemy is unholy, it is best to have holiness on your side for the battle. I assumed that this would be the best course to take; however, I was wrong.

Grandfather took a more fatalistic view of my latest ploy.

"They would first laugh at us, and then they would lock us in the dungeons. This all reeks of blasphemy. Loosed upon the town would come the Inquisition--or worse."

I wondered what was worse than the Inquisitors, but then thought not that long ago I was worried only about some deranged cult who was killing innocent people, and now the undead were first and foremost in my mind--so, yes, things could easily get worse.

We pondered what to do against this new scourge for the better part of the morning, I with an idea, and he with a logical counter. Nothing we came up with truly worked for us. We needed a defense against the vampire, and came up short. Even the traditional defenses of garlic and crosses were (as I was told) meaningless: vampires flee from them only because they believe they should. They have no real power, it is faith that is the true protection; but it must be a flawless faith, and as practitioners of sorcery, we simply do not qualify in that regard. Our very art--once a source of hidden pride for us--was now a nail in the proverbial coffin; for faith demands no knowledge, but we (having knowledge) know the truth beyond reality, and therefore have less faith.

Here is the distillation what we knew about these blood-drinking abominations: they were solitary in their narcissism; appeared alone despising their own kind, yet were at times driven to generate similar progeny; and that there was no force other than true faith that would rebuke their advances.

With that knowledge we agreed, at last, upon this--there was only one such horror against which we must contend; and for that, we were extremely grateful because more than one vampire would be not only an impossibility for men to overcome, but would perhaps show true the end of the world. None would stand against such an arrayed force.

No, Grandfather would think around the issue at hand, and came back again to that which I originated, but I now abandoned as foolish and dangerous.

"Perhaps, against a sole nightmare," he mused aloud. "The light of many may burn away the darkness."

"What?" I foundered, lost in thought.

"With more help, we might be able to trick it, trap it, kill, or drive it away...to a new hunting ground."

"Wait. You thought me insane just a few moments ago for suggesting a fight, now you want to bring others into this? You said we didn't have the power to fight it!"

How is it possible that I had gone from wrong to the polar opposite in such quick succession?

I didn't want to face that thing myself nor along with Grandfather (I feared the worst), even though I believed he might be able to defend himself; even so, it made sense that he would contact others of trust for assistance. Where we lived, and of our order, there were but a few ever, and now even fewer remaining--so in whom could we trust enough to assist in this misguided adventure?

Serendipity strikes at the odd-most of times. It was then that she burst through the door, Juliana, wearing a light dress (not unlike the one she wore yesterday, yet a different color.) Grandfather and I jumped at the shock (she was always demure and an absolute lady in public, but this was no ordinary day, and she in no ordinary mood.) She was empowered by strong emotion, but not broken, not crying. No, she was upset; she was near anger--but not at us. Not at me.

As we blinked at her unbelievable stunt, she shut the door behind her, checking quickly to see if anyone was there (perhaps followed?) Then she whirled and pointed to me, practically ignoring Grandfather, to whom she gave only a cursory greeting (although still polite.)

"What was that thing that took my brother," she was rowdy, boisterous, full of youthful energy, with a bite like vinegar, "And how do we get him back?"

Her well-kept mind could hold back little, and I saw she was on the verge of tears.

I stood in awe, "Juliana!"

My arms slightly open as if in penance before the saints and she rushed forward and held me. Truly, I was in amazement of her appearance here. I wanted to know how she managed come here when I had been told she was ill, but the vision of her as my queen filled my eyes and head and I knew nothing but her heart melting into mine.

And there, again, in my conscious thoughts she was before me as royalty. I was determined that this day-dream would not be made to waste, and within our dream we placed our hands forward as if to touch. But we were blocked by the cold of the glass the separated her from me--the dream-scape was warm and I felt as if I had just come home from a very long and dismal holiday. To me, this was joy.

Grandfather stepped forward, placing hands on both our shoulders, which returned me to unflinching reality.

"Such a brave girl you are," as he stroked the hair at her temple.

He looked at me and I feared his words for I knew what his meaning was.

"We shall have need of such courage."

"You cannot possibly be serious!"

That was the outcome of a discussion that Grandfather, Juliana, and I had almost immediately following her unannounced, dramatic arrival.

Grandfather explained far better than I was able that the being that took Simm away was, in fact, the living-dead--a vampire, and that the deaths up until now--The Doctor and Madame Beck--had been killed by a rogue offshoot of the Holy Church called *Dies Irae*, who wanted to bring down all civilization and authority, and thus destroy man, which in turn would force God to disavow and eliminate his own creation.

He informed her of that which she already knew, that we were practitioners of forbidden arts, and that made us targets for execution in a most grievous manner. She answered that this fact--well, the fact that we were sorcerers--was one of which she was already aware, even if she didn't believe it quite yet (strange tales and curious events do not a sorcerer make.)

As we continued to explain, *Dies Irae* struck hard and fast but would then disappear just as mysteriously as they had arrived. We felt that was the saving grace, if you will, and that with the coming of the undead we were left with just the one task--elimination of the vampire before it chose to remain. Double danger made simpler by the reduction of one.

Grandfather's woeful plan was to use Juliana as a form of bait to attract the creature, then he and I would destroy it using fire and our sorcery before it could escape. As a result of this, the world would (more or less) return to relatively normal: the deaths that had been would be the last.

But as she said, "You cannot possibly be serious! You are not going to use me as some kind of pawn in your game! What if something were to go wrong?"

Grandfather was quick to answer, "We'd take every possible precaution, my dear."

"Don't 'my dear' me! This is insane!"

"You must! There is none else we can trust!" Grandfather pressed on against what I already knew was a losing battle.

"I'll do no such thing!"

I knew that look. She was steadfast, and would not be involved in this scheme. There had to be another way to deal once-and-for-all with a vampire.

"This group, *Dies Irae*, they're gone; and rather than celebrate that, you want to hunt something that shouldn't exist, but does. You're all mad!"

There was a pause for quite a while. To break the uncomfortable silence I asked her how was it she managed to slip away from her home, when I had been told I'd not be seeing her because she was so ill.

"Yes, I was not well this morning; but I am better now. Father was manic, nearly ransacking the entire upstairs! Mother was keen to have me not leave, and locked me in; but I climbed down the trellis from my window."

"You wanted to see me?" I was overjoyed at the prospect of

her desires toward me.

"Yes, well, and your grandfather too. I knew he'd know what happened, and what that creature was. I just didn't expect the story to be so--fantastical. Nor that I was going to be asked to put myself in danger a second time!"

My heart fell a little. I had hoped she wanted to see me, but she wanted information more. Although, I knew in my soul we were bound together. I did not fret the miss-perceived slight.

We sat, all of us, and thought on the (now shared) dilemma. Knowing that these things are predators, that they hunt, and therefore need to find prey in a manner that any other predatory creature might. Grandfather's rejected idea was to make one victim more palatable-- easier to obtain in this instance--than any other perceived food. Vampires are, after all, opportunists, and will feed on that which gives the least path of resistance.

For all our discussion, we could not escape the inevitability of the situation: the confrontation to come would not be in any way, shape, or form like anything we've done, seen accomplished, or even heard about in any manner save the popular folk-tales, which we knew were highly untrustworthy. A sinking feeling of despair toward our future began to arise. Even Grandfather felt it. It was a tangible thing in the room, and the air hang heavy with doubt.

"Are...are you cooking?" Juliana asked shyly.

"No," was my reply. With all the doings and comings of this morning, I had not even begun any preparations for the evening meal.

"Then why do I smell smoke?"

We stared for a brief moment at one another, then in near unison rushed to the door, threw it open, and stepped out into the open late-morning air, where we could see the flames from which the smoke clearly arose.

It was there, up on the hill, down the road, that the flames were seen billowing in the breeze. The conflagration originated from the direction of Juliana's home, it was toward this that she instinctively ran. We knew you could not see the home from here, but there was nothing else in that direction save their mansion. She knew just from the feeling on the wind, intuition if you will, that her family, still inside last she knew, was in an inferno of inhuman proportion.

With fleet feet we (Grandfather and I) closed the distance between the gap that separated Juliana from us; and we caught her. We told her the travel was too great to run, she'd be exhausted by the time she arrived and would be of no assistance.

We must conserve our strength, and walk, not rush. We'd get there in little time; although I feared that long before we arrived, her home would be a shambles of fire, smoke, and debris. True enough, for once we arrived the home was completely engulfed in flame, save a few windows. We three walked into the courtyard through the familiar iron fence; and as soon as she saw the home, Juliana started screaming for her father and mother, and in a panic, rushed to the door, but could not open it, for it was stuck hard. Even with my assistance, the door wouldn't budge.

Stepping back, she pulled her hair back in disbelief, and openly cried.

Actually, "cried," might be the incorrect term I should use. What I witnessed was as if a piece of her soul was wrenched from her body, forcibly: she was in utter agony, tormented by the sight of what was before her. The wails she made cannot be explained other than to say that only one who had suffered so (as she had) could possibly make them.

To hear it, to think of it even now, brings my hairs to stand on end. It was an other-worldly scream that pierced flesh and bone like a knife; and she collapsed to her knees. Her heart aching, she grabbed at her chest, a flood of tears the likes of which no man should see, and no person should ever endure, watered the parched soil beneath her.

I do not lie when I say a piece of her died right there as she knelt on the ground next to the house in which she was born, reared, lived, and loved. I saw a soul shattered like glass, and I, too, wept.

She looked up at me as I stood, "Do something!"

Those two words I wish I could un-hear. This I wished I could undo. I was impotent. There was nothing I could do; and there was nothing I would not do, were it possible, to take from her this pain. I knelt and held her, and she collapsed into me. With no strength in her, she cried--she loosed Hell itself from within her--as all around her the entirety of her world was undone.

We heard the cracking of the wood, bemoaning its burning fate. I pulled her further from the front of the home, lest the wall collapse upon us. She offered no hindrance: like a limp doll she was, eyes wet, shimmering from the flame-light. Her body was here, but in a way she was not.

I heard the cracking of windows, looked up, and saw--something--moving within the upper level of her home. Perhaps there was hope. Grandfather saw it too and gave an utterance to the fact.

"Someone alive!"

Juliana looked up, and there was some hope in her eyes then. Was it her father? Her mother? Unknown. But I did that which I hadn't done in a long time: pray. I prayed one might survive this, if only for the sake of Juliana's sanity.

From the second level, a window's glass was shattered from within, an arm (I think) wrapped in a blanket pushed out the panes--with flames licking at the windowsill from outside, and burning whoever was within. There were screams of anger, pain, sadness, and panic.

It was the voice of her father we heard. In an instant, he withdrew from the window as flames poured out. I thought him certainly slain.

But then he jumped, or perhaps fell, from the window, wrapped head to toe in a badly burned red cloth that fluttered about him as he fell while smoldering. Ultimately, he landed in an inauspicious bundle.

Grandfather rushed to his aid, if any could be garnered. Juliana screamed, "Father!" and rose to her feet and prepared to go to him. I held her back because, plainly, I could see her father was badly burned, horribly injured; and this, I felt, she should not see. She struggled against me as Grandfather knelt beside her father.

He wasn't dead! His arm moved, errant, shaking uncontrollably, as he handed something unseen to Grandfather. His lips moved, but I could not hear what he was saying. Then his hand fell, he arched his back, slumped, and with head to the side he gave up his spirit.

Juliana escaped my bond as Grandfather rose and returned to me. I attempted to grab on to her again, but was rebuffed.

"Let her go to him," he said.

She knelt before her father, gazed upon his broken, scarred, and blistered face. She held him in her arms, and as her hair cascaded down onto his chest she moaned a new soliloquy of anguish the likes of which I hope dearly to never encounter again.

Grandfather walked to me, looking at the thing in his hand. It was well worn, blackened with soot, burned, but still recognizable. He showed it to me once he drew near. It was a clasp for a cloak, perhaps the very one that was wrapped around Juliana's father as he lay.

"What did he say?" I asked.

I looked down at what Grandfather held, and saw a half-circle of brass adorned on top by five equally spaced flames.

"My son's," he quoted in reply.

I quickly turned my eyes back to Grandfather, "Simm was *Dies Irae*?"

"A member, apparently," Grandfather didn't quite believe it himself, but there he was confronted with the evidence directly in his palm.

"Oh, God! Do you think he?..." I was getting at the murders, and my intent was clear.

"Yes, and Juliana need never know this revelation."

On that there was absolute agreement: she must not be told, if it can be avoided.

Our gazes turned to Juliana in her grief; but she was frozen and no longer weeping, for there in the courtyard, just before her, mere feet away low crouched and growling, were three large wolves with hate in their eyes--staring her down--with only her dead father's body between those angry animals and herself.

The wolves were closer to her than we were, and were we to attempt to grab her--to even try to defend her--they would certainly have the opportunity to strike before any move on our part. With the few arrayed folk of the town present, we couldn't use any mystical power to drive the creatures away. A direct confrontation was out of the question, I knew these people--they were not huntsmen of sufficient quality (or quantity) to take on such prey as large as this. Militia would be needed, if not more; and even then, one would expect great harm to come to any that dared.

It was odd to see that these animals, which would never approach this close into town, were now here, and within reach of humans, of whom they ought to be direly afraid. It was as if a will that was not their own had been compelling them and their presence, for their tempo and temperament was not at all like any rational, wild animal that I had ever known. But then, the concept of normalcy had escaped on the winds some time ago.

As I watched, two of the canines were drawing near to her; and she was quite frozen with fear. Their teeth were shown and gnashing. Drool from their mouths made strings that reached near to the soil. With bristling fur this standoff continued for some small while; this was all set against the backdrop of the burning home that continued to creak, moan, and scatter ash and floating embers that fell to the ground like a dirty, first, pathetic snowfall that comes too early in the season.

Perhaps it was the choice of fortune and fate that at that moment a partial wall of the home collapsed in a heap, startling these beasts. This broke everyone's concentration momentarily; and one of the wolves used this moment to lunge forward toward Juliana, but it didn't make it to her: it had been intercepted by one of its brethren.

There ensued a minor scuffle, rolling in the dirt, with whelping and whining, barking and growling. Some blood was shed, fur was torn; and as we watched, a bit baffled by this display, two made a hasty escape and fled to the woods over the low wall that stood on the far side of the home.

The lone remaining wolf, injured, but not beaten, then turned toward Juliana. I had, by this time, crept up towards her and was just behind where she knelt at her father's side. It looked at me, then back to her, and I felt as if the animal was in some manner to me known--or perhaps familiar, even though I am not one to keep ken with beasts-- but I could not say as to why I felt it so. It growled its disapproval, but just as suddenly turned and ran mimicking the actions of the previous two.

It stopped again on the other side of the wall, looking, menacing, angry, and conflicted. But then whelped once, wincing, and with tail between legs ran off as a dog might after hearing the call of an angry master.

Then, we were there, just us and the few onlookers, bathed in the light of the fires that burned. It took nearly an hour for the wood structure to succumb totally, during which time we sat, stared, wept, and wondered what had become of the world.

Grandfather stood there too, watching. I cannot say what he was thinking but if it was anything like what thoughts filled my head and heart, he would know that my first instinct would be to flee our home, even though the nearest village is a week away by foot. But I knew he would brook no retreat now that there were none remaining, except him, that might make a stand against the onslaught of evils plaguing our people.

During all of this, Juliana barely moved at all in my arms. I kissed her softly on the temple and held her tight. Her gaze never wavered once the wolves were gone; she was fixated on the corpse of her departed father. Her mother was most likely still in the home when the inferno befell; surely Juliana was all that was left of that lineage.

We sat seemingly forever. Eventually, after the rafters collapsed, the fire burned down to but a dull shadow of its former self, having burned all available fuel, it was now nothing more than a bonfire of shattered hopes and dreams.

One of the townsfolk walked to what was once the front doorway of the home, and then around to the side of the dwelling, to where clearly what had been once the foyer and kitchens. He was gone minutes only, then returned. I overheard him speak to Grandfather: he had seen some burned and broken bodies.

"Three," he whispered.

That could only mean the remains were of Juliana's mother, the valet, and maid. No more would have been in the home. The circle of family was broken, and what remained of it was now in my arms, cradled, silent, and pawing at the side of her father's face, sitting in a daze brought on by torture I hope to never learn. I turned to Grandfather for support, to see what his kind eyes might give in wisdom as to how to proceed.

"Edouard, what of the girl?" the man asked as I stared.

Grandfather replied matter-of-factually, "She will remain with us. She is our family now."

No-one questioned it. None dared. No heart, even here where appearances may have counted more than the entirety of the wealth of the world, is so cruel as to deny family to their own. They knew, as did any and all who might look, that she and I were bound together.

When Grandfather finally met my gaze, there was no wisdom to share, only pity, remorse, and love. I turned from him, back to Juliana, and held her as close as my arms might muster. Her eyes, her intent, her love, never changed face, never faltered, and never left he whom had given her life; and as if in some sympathetic nature, far away, across the fields, thunder began to roll.

The Earth wept that day as well.

By the time the rains came, we had already returned home, we three unhappy travelers. There was nothing to see and nobody to save at Juliana's former home: it was but a smoldering ruin now. The bodies of her mother, father, and the home-workers had been recovered, graves were dug in their familial plot, and they would be buried that day--rain or no rain. One simply cannot leave such remains out in the open, for the putrid stench of a burned body is particularly unnerving.

As the sole living child, Juliana had inherited everything, which was considerable. Her father had been a very successful merchant and importer of spices from the Orient, and this wealth now resided solely with her. Whereas Grandfather's treasures were in his books, now lost in a peak of paranoia, Juliana's wealth came from gold and silver, of which I am told there was more than enough to last more than one person's lifetime. She would want for nothing.

But money she did not want; and power she never craved. Wealth, for all the luster of gold and gems of the entire world, cannot turn back the hands of time one second; nor can it undo the hurts of the past or return to life those taken from us. It was this that so injured her. Grandfather referred to her state as a form of walking delirium.

Had she been driven (somewhat) mad by the sights of the loss of her family? Personally, I didn't think so, and I held out grand hope that, soon, we might see her return to form, smile again (although this might take a great while and certainly would not come quickly), and hear her lovely voice. Regardless, she could walk, but needed support, and was deeply affected in ways that we could only speculate. Her eyes were focused elsewhere--drawn away from this world by some unknowable force--and dwelt in some twilight realm where the sun did not show from within.

It had taken some doing to extract her from the side of her father. Her love for him was never in doubt--not by him and certainly not by us. Family we were now, and our family we shall preserve.

Though it may break the bonds of the tradition that we should not cohabit in the same dwelling, no person--at least none would be so bold as to mention it--would deign to make their opinion known. For that, I was grateful, as she needed no embarrassment from this arrangement. She needed no insult to her already grievous injuries.

Placing her in my bed so that she might rest, I let her be and returned to the kitchen. Grandfather and I looked long at one another. Communication without words is somatic: one can read faces and the language of the hands and eyes to know intent and feeling. It is not what is called telepathy, but rather empathy for the plight which we shared and with which we were bonded; it is only the most human of conditions that allows for such exchange to exist.

Grandfather sat opposite me at the table, gazing at the oaken planks that supported our daily meals, and sighed heavily in remorse. I was going to ask if nightmares ever end when loosed from the bonds of slumber, but he interrupted my thoughts with words of his own.

"Locarno, they will be coming for me next, you know..."

I hated those words. I hated them because it meant soon he would be gone, and my link to a greater life would be lost with him. I hated them because it meant that *Dies Irae* were winning this war--if indeed we can call this a war at all. Bust most of all, I hated those words because they rang true.

It did not take a powerfully piercing mind to see the pattern: the wealthy, the powerful, the educated, and the elite were all being systematically, methodically, removed--killed-- by the agents of *Dies Irae*. What I didn't understand was how the vampire played into all this, if indeed it played a role at all. I didn't like the happenstance of its appearance and *Dies Irae* at the same time; but as Grandfather explained, as a sect of the Church, even a rebellious one, they would be at direct odds with a being of such malevolence. Together came the apparitions, but together they were not.

"When they come--and they most certainly will--you and Juliana must flee, not fight. You must run, you must escape!"

I looked back at him, "Run? To where?"

"Anyplace your feet take you, but away."

"Can we not fight them together?"

"No, I think not. They would be too strong, and we too few for much resistance."

We talked of such things for a while, until I became tired. I don't know for how long we spoke. Then I retired to my room where I left Juliana in sleep, and thought to myself that I didn't want to have such a discussion again with any person that I found valuable or whom I loved.

How does one prepare for such? How does one say good-bye to family--to resign to the fate that their demise is imminent and you are powerless to prevent it from happening? What good all this secret sorcery if not one piece of it can prevent a greater holocaust?

Damn you, *Dies Irae*. Damn you all to Hell.

As I approached Juliana, she lay turned away from me, still in the bed where I left her. I sat on the edge, careful not to rustle her from her rest, mulling over the discussion I had just left; very much worried about the implications of losing the last member of my family--which although not entirely true, is good enough an explanation considering my mother and father were more strangers to me than actual members of my bloodline.

But she was not sleeping, merely lying there, wordlessly. The silence was then broken.

"They'll be coming for me next."

I was put off by this, as I didn't expect her to speak nor to even think herself the next possible target; and I had just as much said so in reply.

"They killed my family--my brother, mother, father--all gone. I am all that's left. They will close the link; they'll not fail a second time."

To an outsider, it would appear that she and her family was a priority target for *Dies Irae*, but Grandfather and I knew that only her father would have been the true quarry.

I moved to lay beside and behind her, holding her with my arm around her waist, my mouth next to her ear, and whispered.

"I don't think so."

She sighed a little. She didn't think I was being logical, and her breath was a manifestation of her exasperation of my unwillingness to accept her view of the situation. It was remorseful, and she closed her eyes shuddered a bit and cried noiselessly for a brief moment.

"But you have a way beyond this to escape. I do not."

I didn't know in that instant what it was she was on about, and asked her.

"What are you saying?"

With little fan-fare she held up some of the pages of the black book that she had been holding in her unseen hand beneath her body, which she must have easily pulled from my bed. She was specifically holding the pages of the ritual she wanted me to perform earlier. They were crumpled, worn, old, but firmly in her delicate hand and not at all damaged. She held them to me, without turning, and spoke the revelation they held that to her must have been a death-knell.

"Only one can complete this. I was hoping we could together, but two is not one."

I took the pages from her hand, and began to peruse them in more detail. And sure as can be, the words were clear: one may perform, one will turn, one will become. Not two, one.

"You can save yourself by becoming this--I don't even know what the hell it is--"

I interrupted, "I could perform it on you instead."

It was then that she finally, slowly, turned to face me, lying there nose to nose she gave a quaint little smirk. I had amused her, just not in the way that I had hoped.

"No, I'm no sorceress. It takes power I don't have, but you do."

I was willing to sacrifice everything for her, and she rebuked it. I could not deny that she understood the implications of the ritual as well as any who would have read its infernal words. It indeed would take power to perform, and to train her would take far too long.

That's when the logical conclusion of the discussion came to me, and I said it plainly.

"Then I shall do this," motioning with the papers in my hand, "And will do what I can to protect you forever. You are my love, and for you I--"

Her eyes met mine, her lips parted slightly, and she reached up to my face, caressed it softly, and spoke the words that fill a man's heart more than any strong spirit may bring.

"I love you. Marry me."

Since the ancient times, women did not bring forth the cause and question for betrothal. This was the purpose of the male, and I was unnerved by her words. But in the back of my mind, where the silent thoughts slumber, where dreams come from, came forth the vision of her I have when I sleep, adorned in all the finery the world can muster; and her glow was utterly magnificent. I closed my eyes to keep the vision fresh. I saw her there, through the portal, with our hands at fingertips distance. Her smile was a beacon of light in an otherwise dark room. I knew for once and for all time the answer to a question that I, myself, never asked and did not deserve to know.

I purposely opened my eyes, returning to the reality of the moment so I might be clear and carry out that which my heart demands; so that I may speak the words that are inspired within by a power that must have come from outside for my own mortal frailty could not justify the bravery contained within. And with humility, some majesty, and honor I took her hand in mine, leaned toward it, kissed it ever so gently; and with truth on my tongue spoke gallantly in earnest answer.

"We already are!"

And so it was in that moment the bond of our souls became permanent, unquenchable, and felt by us both. None would stand to say we were not wed in that moment, none would dare in my presence, and none would doubt the veracity of our claim.

We are one, heart to heart, soul to soul, in the eyes of the Almighty, from then forward for all time--until the end of the Earth, and possibly beyond.

It was in this manner that I, Locarno, was proposed marriage. Such was it that I gave forth the last full measure of my love; it was in this way, in the sight of none save the Lord God himself, I became husband to Juliana.

And it was made holy by His blessing.

Perhaps it was my effort at love, or perhaps my faith in her, that dried her tears and brought her some measure of joy; it is impossible for me to say much on the subject. All I knew was, with she and I now betrothed her expression changed, practically in an instant, to one of significantly less sadness. It was excellent to see, all things considered.

Yet she was still crest-fallen because of her losses, which is to be expected--her worries were multiple and horrendous. A melancholy still permeated the room as I clave to her unremittingly. With our lips and bodies intertwined, it as if through our passion we would burn through the dark mist that surrounded our lives.

But our love was quickly come to an end, as with all youth it is; and there we lay, together, her head upon my breast as I gingerly ran my fingers through her long, satin tresses. Looking slightly down upon her, it was then I realized something that I had not even known before perhaps in my entire previously-idyllic life: a woman, whom a man loves, need not be grand, she need not be perfection in reality; rather, it is love that makes a woman flawless. If you love a woman, it is your love that renders them ideal.

"I want you to survive this," she whispered. "I cannot bear to have you lost."

I knew what that would entail, and I slowly glanced at the few scattered pages--the ritual--that surrounded our feet at the end of the bed. The grouping lay there, undisturbed, amazingly, from when I placed them there before we coupled for this our second time. The words on the pages mocked me, called to me, and I mourned that I heard them and knew that therein on the written page I was going to be called to my immediate destiny.

"Now?" I asked of my love.

Was it this moment she wanted the process to begin, or rather simply sometime soon? I was in no real mood for magic: I wished only to hold her in my arms and know that though the world was in uproar, there was still good left to be held.

Her warm arms wrapped around me tighter in response, "No, not just yet."

Her devilish smile I could feel as her cheeks pressed against me. I think, for her, this might be a small glimpse of heaven as the hell around us unfolded; and she too wanted to linger in the caresses of our desire, wherein the outside world may not intrude.

In due time we rose from our recline, and dressed as needed, and I rested by sitting on the edge of the bed as the night grew nigh; where there had been bright yellow tinted rays of sun pouring through the high window sill, they had been replaced by the muted colors of early evening. Staring at the pages next to me, I considered them while she tied her dress behind her back, without the use of a mirror, as if she had practiced this particular maneuver in contortion a thousand times. It is a marvel of mechanics, the way a woman can perform these acts that defy the limitations of their own bodies.

She turned when finished, and presented herself to me, her eyes gleamed, and nothing was amiss. She was stunning to look at, even now, even after our deep passion's release. I mouthed to myself that this was my wife, and she showed approval. Even Death itself could not belay her spirit in this moment.

I took up the strewn pages as she straightened her hair and front blouse. The language used was deep German, and very old. I recalled she read some, and was again impressed. I knew she understood Italian, and now German. Her education in languages was clearly superior to many, and perhaps even myself.

"This will take some doing, and sorcery is never a thing with which to trifle."

She looked at me, and I returned the look in wonder. She looked almost hurt by my words. I didn't wish for that to happen and my countenance changed as a result and I quickly reverted.

"But I can do this. Shall we begin?"

Halfheartedly I rose. She smiled a little smile, and pulled the small, blue, glass from the shelf on which it sat, held it out to me (which I took); and I began to intone the words off the ancient parchment. All was in readiness: the vessel, blood of self, and blood of love, and spider's silk was within easy reach. All was prepared, except me, but I was now resigned to fate-for-love, to do that which I said I would--for her whom I loved more than the breath in my lungs, the sky above, and the blood in my veins.

With this I would survive the terrible times which, like a maelstrom, whirled around us, and what I gained I would use to defend those close to me--if indeed I could.

The spell was deceptively simple; some of the most potent rituals are similar: the performance of them can be completed in the blink of an eye, with no outward sign that anything had even occurred; yet no less potent are they, and in many cases are more powerful as a result. As I performed the steps in order, as listed, the very words faded from the page, leaving it blank as if never used. It was a journey of only one direction to travel.

I cut my thumb and bled into the bottle; she pricked hers and did likewise. Spider web was added to draw thin my life--two living souls merged in this arcane way. The bottle was closed with final ceremony with fiery words and ideals of long-past men, which I shall not tell here; then I stood the bottle upwards and projected into it with-- as was commanded--with all force of mind, lest failure be thy final prize.

And in the culmination and crescendo of this--I felt nothing.

I had not changed, I was still myself; yet I knew that something was wrong, but I showed none of this to Juliana, who stood faithfully by as witness. Though I had no outward change one could see or feel, I knew that there was something at work within. I understood something. I felt Juliana. She and I were as one, and there was another soul I knew: another bonded by love and blood.

I turned, looked to her, and I knew that which she had not revealed. I knew she was with child. Our Child. My child. My heart swelled with great gladness.

I could feel it within her. I could sense its presence in the room just as I felt Juliana near me. What consequences unforeseen this may have I did not know. The ritual was certain: two perform, and no more. I worried about the implications.

She must have seen my face, and I stopped. I chose to deftly hide what I knew, and sheepishly spoke.

"Sometimes the magic works, and sometimes it does not."

She laughed just a little, but I knew there was some pain in her soul then. She felt I was endangered as well, and the loss could be terrible to take. She asked how I felt. I explained I felt fine, as if nothing had changed at all.

"Perhaps I misread something," again I hid what I knew.

We embraced, and I felt both their souls in my arms.

Following that, we placed the blue phial up on my top shelf and wondered what will become of us now.

We did not have long to wonder, for it was just then, mere moments in reality, that a commotion could be heard in the other parts of the home. I heard crashes, yells of anger, growls of unintelligible natures, and whispers of hideous scents coming from under the door and around its cracks.

Juliana held to me, but I knew we must go out; we were trapped here, and to see what was happening--to assist if needed--for only we three were in the home earlier; now there were others, and a quarrel of great ferocity had ensued.

I opened the door, and here and there on the floor I could see the strewn refuse of the struggle: pots, pans, broken dishes, overturned chairs, and our dinner table's shattered top lay in a pile of wood only suited for kindling.

I smelled the overpowering stench as soon as I opened the door. My eyes filled with stinging water, and I held my nose against it. At least I could breathe through my mouth. I knew this nastiness from before, for once you encounter it, you know it intensely and will carry its memory with you for your entire life. Like the scent of the dead it stays with you forever.

There was a vampire in my home. I nearly retched then, just as before, but remained composed. What good would it do to vomit on my shoes when escape was the paramount concern, even if it was reactionary and unintentional.

Grandfather backed from his study into the kitchen, where I could see him. He was loosing mystical bolts of flame like a burning torch before him as he retreated, preventing the unseen, but not un-smelled, creatures from advancing. Intermittently he'd curse them in a foreign tongue I didn't recognize, they would howl; then he would unleash his particular brand of flame at them, and would step back, further away from the things that have no place in the order of Creation.

Yes, there were two here; and he confronted them both, and was somewhat successfully holding them at bay. It was then, and only then, did I realize that Grandfather was a man of extremely potent power. I could easily imagine him defeating one; but to hold two at a distance, and to not even seem to be bothered too much by the effort, showed that he was, without a doubt, a sorcerer of supreme capability. This was a side of him that only an inkling of which were even shown prior. I stood momentarily in absolute awe of the spectacle he unleashed.

"Grandfather!" I cried out.

"Locarno? Get out of here! Run!"

I mustered up what I could in a form of courage--and make no misunderstanding of this--the amount of courage needed to charge out into a room occupied by disgusting creatures emitting smoke and an aura of evil is not something I wish to do again in my long life. But it was needed, and so I went.

Juliana and I crept carefully out of the door into the open. I watched the vampires try to weave a mist around them to obscure their bodies. Grandfather was no fool, and was keen to their plans, and he kept burning and cursing them. I don't know what he was saying, but I found it extremely odd that the fire they seemed to shrug off rather easily; rather his words were causing them harm somehow. It was only when he cursed at them did they howl. What it was he said, had power. Great power.

I wanted to help him, and I readied a spell I had learned but not used. Grandfather used fire already, and wishing only to make their appearance in our home less hospitable--they were after all not our guests--I called forth something I had only practiced once, and I prayed I would be more accurate with this than with any spell I had tried before.

Lightning shot from my fingertips then struck into the room past Grandfather's shoulder and head. He turned quickly at me, glancing only, with a look of startlement. One of the shadows from the other room retreated from view.

"Locarno! Run, boy! You must flee!"

I ceased my casting, and I do not know if the spell hit anyone or anything, but it cast great arcs of light and shadow as it went, and it was so close to Grandfather it made his hairs stand on end, lightly scorching some of his speckled mane. There were flashes and I heard a crashing, and there was some smell in the air--not one I had encountered before, almost mechanical; I set forth a beautiful sight of rainbow hues, mostly in the white and blue spectrum, cut short by Grandfather's command and my loyalty to him.

"Run!" He echoed his command.

"Grandfather, come with us!"

"I'm trying!" His reply was as obvious as it was glaringly impossible.

To the door we (Juliana and I) went, and I opened it. That was our unfortunate mistake. We were safe where we were, and having given the enemy an opportunity for a second front of assault, they took the initiative.

Juliana screamed when it was flung open. There stood one of those beasts. Either another, or it was one and the same that had disappeared from the room when I cast my shocking flare.

I saw on this one a great smoldering scar on his face, freshly carved, which I could only hope hurt in ways that only few can attest. I pushed Juliana back and retreated. She held my arm with strength only the mad or scared to wits-end can possess.

Grandfather turned to see our progress and saw we were at a standoff against a creature we could not handle. That's when he was attacked and fell, screaming all the way down. The near creature's breath knocked us to the floor like a foul wind; and as we attempted to scramble back into my room, it grabbed our ankles and dragged us toward him. With his maw open and dried blood falling like sand from his mouth he reached for us, one of his hands was upon my mouth and one grasped Juliana's face.

Struggling against that level of strength is impossible. I glanced only quickly at Grandfather, and screamed a mortal scream into the paw-hand of the beast. It was muffled, and few, if any, would hear it.

I could not breathe. The hairs on the hand filled my mouth and nostrils. I saw Grandfather on the floor unmoving, being dragged away. I turned back to the beast above me, the last thing I saw was its eyes: the bitter blue eyes hidden by a face that was not man, nor beast, but somewhere in between. With the ruffled, fringed, upturned nose of the bat, and powdered and dried blood falling from its open mouth, making the whole scene ever the more menacing.

It was then I began to lose consciousness, the last thing I remembered was the equally muffled screams coming from Juliana, who was on my right, laying on the floor just as I. Then all went black. I saw nothing, heard nothing, felt nothing. The nightmare, at least, was over; they had come for us all--Juliana, Grandfather, and myself. As the darkness became absolute and control and consciousness left me I knew the entire world was going to soon be equally dark as my vision in the long decades to come.

Screams.

That's what I heard. It is no fallacy that when a person loses consciousness the last sense to leave, and the first to return, is their hearing. Before I could even wince an open eye, I heard them, those horrid screams.

The screams, somewhat luckily, weren't mine. But unfortunately, I knew from whom they emanated; and I didn't like it one bit.

They were Grandfather's screams.

Groggily, I lifted my head and forced open my eyes, and tried to focus my wavy vision. I found that my arms were bound by shackles on chains above my head, bolted to the stone wall at my back. Across from me, about a man's length away, on the opposite wall, similarly bound, was Grandfather. He was screaming, eyes ablaze, bloodied, badly beaten, being burned and branded.

Before him stood the vampire, draped in red, brandishing the sickly orange-red hot branding iron deep onto Grandfather's chest. Pushing, turning, twisting, and peeling flesh, inflicting hideous pain. I could see the skin rip and tear and burn underneath the undead's dreadful strength. This was the same vampire, the one with the blue eyes--the one with the scar--the one that choked Juliana and I as we lay on Grandfather's floor. At least I could no longer smell the beast. My nose, I think, was broken, a small favor, perhaps. A bit painful but a welcome favor none-the-less.

Once my senses returned more fully, I tried to kick at the beast, but could not reach. The long legs I had were not enough to bridge the distance. I tried to pull against the chains, but iron is not forgiving. I grunted and pulled all to no avail.

"Leave him, you fiend!"

That was all I could muster, and I feared that all it did was make it aware that I was now awake. Surely I would be next on his torture regimen.

It threw down the brand, now cold, the flesh had melted to its steel, and it tore a path from Grandfather's chest as it fell. More screams. More hideous, terrible screams.

Grandfather lifted his head back, showing some sign of resolve within. He looked at me with his kind eyes and the love I had come to expect and always feel.

"Locarno..."

He could barely speak, the hoarseness of his throat caused, no doubt, by the unending wails he was made to produce in his unrelenting torment. Their pleasure; his torment.

He followed with deep breaths and something I will never forget, "I was wrong. Look..."

With that, he glanced at the vampire, wanting my eyes to follow where his went. I did not know what he saw nor what it was he wanted me to see; I could not know what he wanted me to know. The beast was not facing me. I looked back to his eyes and must have shown despair or confusion--or both.

I heard a shushing, a gurgling, a retching. The beast's mouth opened and spoke in a tone I had heard long before. It brought back memories of a time when Grandfather and I had been visited by a friend from the North, from the lands of the fjords (as they called them.) It was a warm summer then when he came to us, that friend of Grandfather's. At the time, the visitor's accent drew images in my mind of sweeping forests and snow covered mountains. Clearly this once-human beast was from the North as well--he was a Norseman--and his thick accent was made thicker by the vocalizations that only a vampire could produce.

"Now I can take my pleasure of you!"

Nothing more chilling could come forth from that thing--or so I thought.

It did not take long for me to be proven wrong in that brief belief, for from its open maw extended a bestial tongue the length of which would defy logic. It was thick, mucousy, glistening, and altogether disgusting; and with its flopping, muscled, broken swaying rhythm, it became a new weapon against Grandfather, replacing the iron brand that now sat on the floor at their feet.

The length of the tongue rose up to Grandfather's face. He tried to turn away from it, but he could not. I could hear him grimace vocally against it as it writhed on his face, coiling like a snake, leaving slight trails and pock-marks where its surface met him. Like an octopuses arm it was, but with invisible suckers pulling on his forehead and cheeks, and when it pulled away leaving small blood droplets that it had brought to the surface, which were quickly wiped away--absorbed by other parts of the tongue.

As Grandfather squirmed, the tongue forced open his mouth--the vampire taking great pleasure from the sight--and it slid into his mouth. Grandfather's eyes opened wide as the thing slid deep into his mouth, choking him, suffocating him. He retched as his reflexive gagging came into play, but there was no release. The vampire stepped closer, and watched eye-to-eye as Grandfather was violated. Down the throat I could see the tongue crawl, leaving bulges here and there as it went; and the vampire, as well as it could, all things considered, smiled a wicked grin as the tongue bored and probed its way down the throat--

toward Grandfather's heart.

I struggled against the chains even more, with what might I could muster, and it was to no conclusive result. I yelled, trying to distract the thing from him. I locked eyes with Grandfather's and cried out; and the evil thing kept driving the probing, pulsating tongue deeper.

Grandfather's screams were muffled forever and his eyes went dim all in one instant when the tongue reached the center of his chest, tore through his windpipe from within, and grasped a hold of his heart like an apple, cracked it open, draining in seconds all the life's blood he contained. Grandfather went pale, slumped; and his head would have slacked under its own weight had it not been held up by the strength of that creature's vile exploration.

This is what it is like to see one of these abyss-dwellers feed; this is how they destroy. This is how my Grandfather, my friend, my mentor--my family--perished: a soul of infinite kindness extinguished by something diametrically opposed to life. In my soul I said a prayer, and made a vow. Were I able, this thing I would do for all time: I named them Enemy--forever. When such a time of revenge would come, there would be no mercy, even if the world should be made to burn.

The reverse of the process--the pulling back--caused little to be seen, which is a blessing, except that upon leaving the mouth blood was left caked around Grandfather's lips. It was then it all came unto me, and the beast turned slowly, and I could see the entire picture in full view.

The caked and dried blood on the mouth, the branding on the chest, and now the broach-clasp that this creature wore that held his cloak which I could now plainly see: there were not two plagues upon us, *Dies Irae* and the vampire; rather, they were one and the same. This was Grandfather's mistake; this was his moment of failure.

Dies Irae and the undead were one and the same.

Screams.

The stone walls echoed with screams. This time, however,
they were mine as I watched, helpless, as Grandfather died--right there
before my eyes--and I could do nothing to save him. My eyes filled
with tears. I could not breathe. There was a lump in my chest that
moved to my throat. I wailed. I hated. I feared. I was destroyed.

Just as Juliana's world was undone previously, so too now was
mine. Death came, I saw it. It drained his color, his blood; his flesh
made white. His eyes turned dim and fell; and his last breath, warm and
moist against the cold air, made vapor as he exhaled: just as his soul
departed for all time.

Howling like an animal injured, I closed my eyes. I could see
nothing but his precious face--the memories of his great life--his
greater lessons--brought forth in my soul a pain I cannot understand.
May you never learn it fully yourself.

I could not think, my mind raced and was equally stopped as
if by an unseen force. I knew, I felt, only pain of what was there once
before me; within me I was nearly turned inside-out. This vision boiled
up bringing more of the love I remembered, making this worse by the

very second. There are many words for suffering, and none of them would suffice.

A soul forever extinguished. I called to God the Almighty. All was horror. My mind fled. There was nothing I could do. I pulled against the chains to get to Grandfather; they would not yield to me. Iron kept me from him. Iron, a metal--unfeeling, uncaring, remorseless iron. I railed against the chains, each time pulled back to the wall with concussive force on the stone and mortar. Physically, I felt none of it.

I made a cry that came from within, I felt myself slacken at the knees. My voice turned hoarse, and my tunic was wet with spit and tears. If only I could have reached him!

Pulling, screaming, dying from within, I wept bitter tears. If a man can be made a shambles of a being, such sight and emotion can surely bring it to fruition from inside. Were love between family a silver cord, as the tales tell, then both suffer equally when it is cut.

I heard clicking of chains--Grandfather's shackles--as he slumped as far as he could, then hung there by the wrists, taut, head bowed down, knees slack. A rag-doll came to mind. Bowing nearly in twain as he went down: a marionette held fast by the strings. But he was no puppet; he was a man, a mentor--family. He was a greater part of me than can be known, and as he fell forward his palpable death-rattle brought forth an echo in the chamber; and each tick of it was a shock to all who may behold the sound.

All this in seconds, and the pain of my soul made it into a thousand years.

"Grandfather?" I cried to the sky in utter agony.

There was no answer. There could not be. No reprieve from God. How could there? There was nothing to stand before me as angel or prophet to come forth to spare him. Mine was a world of darkness, and my soul shattered at the sight. Pain from within cannot be denied: none are so fierce to hold sway against such.

My hands shook, I was choked. Bile, I tasted blood and bile, stinging in my throat. My chest ached. It arched through me, I breathed hard. Heartache such that one might think it would stop beating altogether. And were it to do so, at least my suffering would end as well.

"No!" I lamented further.

There can be no denial. No end of it. Nothing could stand against the truth of this. Grandfather was not so much fallen from that *Great Precipice* of life, rather he was thrown.

Horrendous noises I cannot explain came from me. A wail, a bawl; a mournful, wicked whimper emanated from depths within me deep as the oceans--all of these and more for which there are no words. Salt stung me, a grievous wound from within: now I was he who was without hope.

My mind thought of blasphemy, I asked myself *Where, Lord, are you? Why have you abandoned me? Was I not faithful unto you and your Holy mission? Why allow this to happen? Are you impotent against this evil as well?*

As my heart bled and poured out all there was to fulfillment, the vampire watched, grinning in a way that only one so deformed could do. He held his intention on me, feeding from my sorrow and sadness in some fetid manner. Through me and my suffering he was invigorated. It was intoxicating to him--witnessing my pain and sorrow.

As I poured out my soul in torment, he took greater and greater pleasure from my lachrymose and dismal display. His blue eyes flashed in the torchlight like a beacon themselves.

He laughed a deep, low, grave-like cackle. Short, yet clear it slowly wafted through the room.

"Ahhh!" It sniffed, as if my agony was something the air could carry.

Perhaps it is; perhaps they can see it, feel it, observe it as a breeze is captured by a sail and propel a ship at sea. It was to him a hearty finish to a glorious meal.

There was no glory for me. I was at an end, and in my depression cared not if this beast fed from me in unkind manner. Just as

Grandfather's, my soul was dead as well, and the noise it made within me made physical manifestations in my bones and I shook, slumped as far as I could, and let loose from within the last curse of a noise that can be made by a man. I was numb. There was a buzzing in my ears. I hurt, but not from physical pain.

I knew how Juliana felt, I understood her horror, her losses, her pain and sorrow; and it utterly destroyed within me all there was.

Of Juliana, I could not see, nor hear, any sign.

As my unfortunate wails crawled slowly to a semblance of silence, I cried out to Juliana, hoping she may be near--she, my love, my soul, my world. I had been responsible for dragging her into this scenario. The blame for her shed life, if she was no longer living, lie squarely with me.

"Juliana!" I let out a whimper as I hung there, suspended by those wrist chains.

It is a little known fact that sorcery cannot be performed when ones hands are bound, manual and physical expression and freedom is needed. Woe that it was true, else Grandfather would have dispatched the foul beast with ease and we would hastily have made an escape.

It was just then that I heard something off to my right. It was unseen, and I couldn't say what it was, but it felt familiar. I hearkened again to it, and then I learned it: Juliana was lightly moaning, as if she was waking from a drunken night of terrible slumber.

She was alive! Oh, dear God! She lived! I heard her fine voice and called again. In my breast, the heavens sang and I knew some semblance of hope again.

"Juliana?" There was no reply but moans.

With some strange boldness, from whence it came I do not know, I straightened a bit and struggled. The vampire watched as I rose slowly, curiously his smirk--if one can call it that--never left his face. Hope was on my lips and his feast of my emotions never lessened because of it.

I called her name again, "Juliana!"

Then I turned to him, that disgusting, murderous, life-leeching thing, and dared raise my tone.

"What have you done with her?"

This, the vampire did not like, not one bit. Its grotesque visage changed from a smile, to one of disgust. Then anger. Hope, it seems, is an effective weapon against them in some manner; either that or it was just that I deigned it permissible to speak to him in that way. Regardless, that anger would soon turn to action.

I heard a slight whimper from her, calling my name.

"Locarno..."

I turned to the sound. All the while, the vampire drew his short blade from his scabbard and stepped forward slightly. I heard the withdraw it made against the leather sheath, but my mind did not pay it heed as it should have done.

It spoke, using that same disgusting, wind-forced tone of Northman death from before.

"I have no use for you, whelp!"

Stepping forward, he plunged the blade into my stomach, lifting me up and supporting my entire weight on it, lunged forward sinking the steel blade into the wall behind me.

The gnawing, tearing, rending flesh of my belly was on fire. I moved to scream, but could not. The air would not move in my lungs. I clamped my eyes closed. I saw white. There were flashes of warmth and a chill unbounded. I felt weak. The numbness I had so earlier felt was no more as every fiber of my being screamed out in pain. I felt wetness on my pants as blood poured down and tinted them that unmistakable magenta stain.

The white I saw drew away at the corners of my vision, replaced by darkness; and I heard Juliana's voice call my name yet again.

"Locarno?..."

It was clearer now, even as my hearing began to fade into silence.

Then the vision came to me as she cried out thrice my name in horror. There I stood again, in my daydream, as I see her when I close my eyes and think of us: her in finery, crowned, with infants at her feet; I on the other side of a portal of cold glass viewing her as she stands. Arms of us both raised as we touched fingertips at its flat, smooth, glass surface. I heard the babies coo, then cry, and then they were made silent. I looked at her feet, and they faded from view, replaced by nothing--as if they never were.

I looked up again to her, and she back at me. Her expression changed from gladness to sorrow. Her hair darkened, the light dimmed, and her gown and crown were replaced by simple clothing as the finest furs she once wore were no more.

The vision then changed even as I attempted to struggle to her, I could not move. My spirit, if I can call it that, flew, then I saw, and I knew and I understood what I had been seeing all those many times, and my mind was torn by the revelation. My soul cried out. Sadness, sorrow, death. Hell and all things passed through me as I learned, finally, the last measure of the secret that this vision portended.

It was not I on the other side of the glass; rather, it was her reflection. She was seeing herself in a mirror. I was she, and she was in turn seeing only herself there. She viewed herself as this royalty only because of me: My love made her this regent, and now, somehow, this changed and she was no more *The-Queen-As-She-Is*, but was lessened. She was still Juliana, but diminished and saddened and less.

I hated the turn this vision made. I felt no pain now. All was blissfully calm within me; but the vision, still in my head, having turned so sour filled me with anger. Rage. I saw red. The color filled me, my eyes, my heart, my mind--all red.

Opening my eyes, I heard a rush and sound of the world came back. Looking down, I saw the sword that held me pinned to the wall, my feet were a foot from the ground, a pool of my blood on the floor. Reaching down with my bare hands, I grabbed the blade and pulled it with great ease from the wall and I dropped, splashing scarlet droplets in arcs around my feet.

"No!" I cried. "Bring it back! Bring it back!"

Pulling the blade from my body, I felt nothing. Still seeing a glowing red, I turned it in my hands and grasped it by the grip above the pommel. Lifting my eyes, I saw the vampire before Juliana, who moments ago had screamed my name, now silently standing-- unmoving as if in a dream.

Quickly, I moved to behind the beast as it turned to face me. It looked at me with those cold, dead, blue eyes filled with unnatural life; at first it saw me as I ought to be seen--just a boy, barely a man, a meal with a little fight left in it--but then its expression changed to one of abject, absolute horror as I lofted the blade high and brought it down upon its exposed neck.

Faster than it could blink, in a blur, I wielded it like a hammer. It sliced through his gullet at an angle, from the left to the right, to just below his arm, front to back sliced through. His body was made in twain.

As the top of him fell and the rest of his body began to slump, I changed position of the blade in my hand, and came down with it, and staked the creature through his gaping mouth to the hewn rock floor; and as the hilt was pushed through to his parted lips I let out a ghastly primal scream which made the rock crack beneath him, his eyes turned white and rolled back into his head, and his face instantly desiccated and dried forming deep pockets of dry wrinkles everywhere. A foul wind blew shortly thereafter and his stench permeated the air no more as the thing's essence was extinguished for all time.

As I watched its force of life wash away, I thought to myself damnation upon it: Let Hell itself be his final reward.

I turned to Juliana. My red vision faded to white clarity tinted with blue. She stood there in a daze, mesmerized by the slain vampire, no doubt; I touched her precious face, whispered to her to awaken, which she groggily did. I then winced in absolute pain, and then fell in a lump at the feet of the woman whom I loved.

As I have no earthly recollection of some of the next events that happened, I can only speculate. I do know that sometime later I semi-awoke, on my bed, back in my home.

I have fleeting visions as I passed in and out of consciousness. Juliana must have--somehow--managed to get me home. I have a vague memory of being told, by her, to walk as she supported my weight with my arm over her shoulder. I know it was a warm day. I remember the tall grass at my feet as I stumbled and screamed from the unending pain. As I saved her from the vampire, she now--and with great effort--attempted to save me in return.

There are memories of blood. Lots of blood. Everywhere. Draining down my body to my shoes, my feet were soaked in it--the blood was clearly mine.

Amazingly, once home, she prepared a poultice for my gaping wound, and wrapped it in cheesecloth about my midsection. There was soup that she made, or obtained either from materials we had still in our cupboard or purchased at the marketplace. Though the bowl sat on my nightstand, I'm not sure whether or not I managed to eat any.

Sleep was impossible, but I fell into and out of awake states alternatively almost at whim, which is rest enough, I suppose. The room was either too cold or too warm at any moment. Thankfully, she was my loving caregiver. Several times, when I was shivering, she would lie next to me and hold me to keep me warm. Even the sun wasn't enough to warm me when it passed through the window.

At least I remember pieces, which is better than nothing at all.

I thought in my delirium I heard a commotion in the kitchen, a scream. I wasn't sure. I couldn't rouse myself. I was trapped to my bed and I was very much sleepy. It was like a dream, vision clouded, sounds highly distorted. I really wasn't sure what was going on; and all I could do was lay and moan.

Pain was my constant companion. It shook me to the bone, to my core. The sword that stuck me to the wall, though sharp still only tore rather than cut. The wound was terrible and it bled almost continually. Were it not for Juliana's assistance, I would not have been in any shape at all that was fit for survival.

I blacked-out often. Visions of a feral face peering at me from beyond the door were haunting me and made me nauseated further.

In time, I began to feel somewhat better. The pain had subsided. The poultice was working, I thought. I wonder what herbs she used. This would be valuable knowledge to have for the future, should I need it again. I wasn't hungry, but that was probably for the best as one should not eat with a abdominal wound. More than once had I heard tales of a person doing so and the injury becoming septic, and later the unfortunate person died. I'd rather avoid that fate if I was able.

When night finally came, and on again until nearly morning, I tried, as I said, to sleep, but could not. Though it was dark outside, my room was all lit with a blue glow. I blamed the moon for this. The subtle hues of the night can still be frighteningly blinding until one's eyes totally adjust.

I tossed and turned as well as I could, trying to cover my eyes for rest. It was maddening. I saw its brightness always. I called to

Juliana asking what the light was and if she could remove it.

There was no reply and she was not next to me. Frustrated, I sat up to try to locate the source of my annoyance. I looked to the window. The moon was there, sure, waning as it ought; but not bright enough to be the impetus of my nocturnal issue.

Glancing around the room, I scanned to see if she had found, perhaps, one of Grandfather's candles. It was possible that one might have been enchanted in some fashion to produce a colored light. He was a collector of the strangest odds-and-ends, so it was not without precedent for such to be present.

No candles and no new, burning log on the fire in the hearth. And Juliana was not to be seen.

"Juliana?" I called carefully.

Had she left? Where would she go? Was she safe?

I stood, weakly at first, but soon strength returned and I was able to walk. I looked at my shirtless torso, tightly wrapped with the hasty work of bandaging Juliana must have produced. There was some dried blood that had been pulled to the surface, but otherwise my wrappings were clean and relatively well maintained. She'd done an excellent job, and I was fortunate to have such a skilled woman as wife.

I stepped carefully into the kitchen, it was a shambles. Pots and pans lying around, mostly still the mess from when we were all abducted. There was signs of fire-damage to the walls and deep marks in the wood flooring. I could smell rotten food from somewhere. I'd have to locate that and dispose of it at some point, but not now, as I had other concerns with which to occupy my mind.

"Juliana?" I called again, this time with a little more concern and strength of voice.

There was no reply. My words echoed into Grandfather's library and study. There was none here save myself, and no explanation as to the source of the light that filled my room when all other rooms were dark, dank, and empty.

Shuffling back to my bed, I looked to see if I could locate the light. Using my body as a guide, I noticed shadows. Then I turned and looked up to the point opposite the casting.

There was the source. There, on my top shelf, just as I had left it, just as I had placed it a day (or more, as I couldn't be certain how long it had been) ago was the blue phial we used for the oil for our bread on our excursion in the field the day we discovered Madame's corpse. High on the shelf it sat, and glowed with a light all its own.

I reached for it and pulled it down. I could see into it nothing but a spark within that produced a light with no source of fuel or heat. The stopper was sealed as I had when completing the ritual.

This was my soul. It had been transferred to the phial. The ritual, somehow, had actually worked.

I knew, in that instant, that I was now no longer countable as one of the living. I had become that which the ritual called "Leiche," "cadavru," "corpse": I had become what was in our tongue a Lich, a living embodiment of Death.

"Oh, my God!"

As I stood there, holding the glowing, blue phial, I was mesmerized, enthralled, attached, and drawn-in to the beauty of it all. It almost sang to me, in a chorus of harmony, light and sound; rhythms of seemingly orchestrated filaments of gold, white, blue, and other colors swarmed, pulsed, and swayed.

When I touched the glass, the wisps within reacted--it reached out to me, to where I came closest, charming me, haunting me, pulling toward me, glimmering, wishing to be physically held, touched, caressed, loved, wanted, and needed. I could almost perceive it wanting to come home, into me again, calling me. It buzzed like an insect in flight in my ears, obscuring all other sound.

There was no light in the room, save this, and that was all I needed; there was no need for more! All my world faded away, all I needed was right there in the glass, echoing my name. Blissful was the time I spent staring at the marvel that it was, and I cared not for the outside world anymore: only this, my soul, once covered in the cowl of my body, now free at last to dance and bask in its own light, to play in the open air.

I and my soul were one as I stared at it in disbelief. I was giddy with it, like a drunken man. We danced around the room in a daze together, the phial and I. There was warmth that emanated from it in a way I cannot explain; in my hand the glass was like fire and ice-- there was no burning sensation, nor was it cool. It was explosive, like fresh cut mint and cinnamon spice from the far reaches of the world.

I could smell it--a warm hearth, a burning log with balsam. It filled my lungs, and were my heart still beating in my chest, it would leap in joy and love--my love was reflected in the glass I held. It was the dearest thing on the Earth, and nothing more could be so precious than this moment which I hoped would stretch on for eons without end.

Scratches and whines at the periphery of my mind came in. From whence they came, I do not know, but I blotted them out: they were unimportant, nothing was of import save this, and the world could drag itself into perdition for all I cared, this moment was mine alone!

Soft sluggish beating came from the phial, like a drum and fife in unison--there was no measure to it, simple coy cries with a voice from beyond. I stared at it with blank abandon and felt myself begin to slip away into unfettered ecstasy.

Pounds, scratches, growls, yelps intruded into my mind from outside our unison. What clever ruse the world had to play to draw me from my attraction. I wished it no heed and begone.

Back to my delirium I willfully went and nearly I and it were one again when the pounding, snarling, aching from the door came rushing like a tidal-wave of sound, pummeling all resistance away, washing out of my mind to clarity. I was incensed.

Setting the phial--the lovely phial--back on the shelf, I stormed to the door and threw open the latch and with vigor and a voice like a barbed briar cried out.

"What?"

And there, cowering before me, head bowed, eyes fixed upon me, parchment packet in its mouth, was a large wolf--curiously familiar. It whimpered, tail drawn beneath it in some fashion of fear and duty.

I could make out only part of what was written on the packet held firmly in its jaw.

...Lord...

The beast was sent as messenger-carrier. I looked at it, and it at me; our eyes met. There was some friction there.

Reaching for the message it carried--clearly for me--it snapped a little, growled, but just as quickly whimpered and winced in pain. Controlled, it was, by the alien will of its master to do this task against its better nature to flee or fight. The wolf wanted to bite and run, it was filled with great trepidation, and shook like a spring new-budded leaf in the misty morning breeze.

Taking the letter, which it did relinquish to me, albeit begrudgingly and only after it had been reminded again with a wince of what duty it was to follow, I stood and read the words on the exterior for the first time.

To The Dread Lord

"Lord?" is that what they call me, I wondered.

I opened the package, and began to read the contents, all the while the wolf did not move, did not flinch, did not flee, and its eyes never left me at any time.

Unholy Lord,
PEACE we bid unto thee. That is what we
desire, only PEACE between us. We have her,
and shall not harm her, nor her most precious
life within. Release yourself from this place
and we shall release her unto you as well.
Flee, and know PEACE.

As I read the words, I knew full well what they entailed. I dwelt upon them, especially the last--peace.

Peace--accord, amity, armistice, cessation, conciliation, concord, friendship, love, neutrality, order, pacification, pacifism--the words echoed in my mind like a hammer on a nail.

Peace--reconciliation, treaty, truce, unanimity, union, unity, harmony, agreement--I could think of nothing but these as I clenched my jaw and my vision began to flare.

Peace--amicable, at peace, calm, conciliatory, diplomatic, friendly, gentle, neutral, peace-loving , peaceable, peacemaking, placatory, placid, quiet, serene, tranquil, untroubled--in my mind they drilled like an awl into wood. I clenched my fists. The wolf whimpered. I let out a slight cry of torment.

I knew what they were doing; they had enchanted the words, to delude me, to obfuscate things, to eliminate my mind. To take from me my one chance, to hold over me what there was as their only bargaining point: Juliana. They sought to harm me with mystical powers written here that I had unleashed upon my unsuspecting self.

"Juliana!" I pierced their veil of darkness with her name.

Focusing my strength of will I obliterated their rogue assault and purged it with my own consciousness honed by my desire for her; and as the words, which repeated endlessly over and over in my mind, stopped in a snap like sinew cut with a knife, my eyes opened, and the wolf nearly jumped because of it. It had watched the whole event transpire, unmoving, unflinching, until now when I brought forth my mind to clarity.

I looked at the wolf, and with fire in my eyes, seeing red, I called forth a flame from within, and the parchment I held burst into sickly green flames as I cast it to the ground. The wolf watched in horror, the light reflected in its unmoving, unblinking eyes.

"Lord?" I mocked the letter to the wolf. "That is what they call me, yet assail my person!"

"Peace?"

Again I accused toward the wolf, their emissary by proxy.

"This they say, with no pity!"

"They call me--they dare to call me--unholy!"

I shook with rage. The world was red, my sight was blinded by the color, which tinted everything the hue. Even from behind me, red flooded the room, even as the sun, rising in the East, poured through the doorway from beyond where the wolf stood, cowering. The rays of the sun itself could not wash away the light of my emotion as it conjured within me dark tales of woe upon those that dared touch Juliana's flesh.

The wolf wanted to run, this I could see. It was highly agitated and very uncomfortable in my presence, and I only barely wondered if I were somehow emanating something that was making it so; but it did not flee, it stayed as if bolted unto the ground at the entryway.

"Here is a message for you to return to your masters!"

I pointed my finger at the animal, which cried and crawled backwards only a little.

"Tell them--"

In the middle of my thought, a new one came to me. A delightful new thought that destroyed the bile-laden diatribe I was to unleash.

"No..." I said, and the wolf shook and whined. "I have a better idea!"

With speed that was beyond the wolf's ability to even detect or react against, in a blur, I reached out with one arm, and grabbed the animal by the scruff of his neck and lifted it high up onto the sill of the door, to my eye level.

It cried out in pain, growled, moved as to get away, but could not. I had a grip like that of death upon it and it could not free itself. Its hind-legs making pitiful scratches into the wooden floor beneath as it raced for traction with which to make its dearly desired escape.

With its legs flailing, I held the beast steadfast to the wall and gazed into its open eye. I could feel its heartbeat in my hand, I could see its fear in its eye, I could do anything I wanted. This beast was mine.

"Tell me where they are!"

My mind, like a drill, poured into his. Its psyche was no match for mine as I bored through his feeble resistance with the ease of a hot knife through warm butter. It winced, cried, yelped in pain. I cared not for the feelings of this thing as I stormed through the mind of the animal, looking, searching, pillaging like the raiders of old searching for treasure through the formerly hidden confines of the beast's intellect. It shook ferociously and tried to bite, but I held it strong and just as it gave up its secret that I wanted so dearly, it let out a final yelp that echoed across the meadows and streams, across the fields and trees, and to wherever they may have taken her--to wherever they may be hiding--and I hoped they heard it and it made their skin crawl.

      I knew they heard it, and the sound was like music to my revenge filled un-beating heart.

The beast's mind had bent to my will, but not without unfortunate consequences: it simply could not survive the assault and as its mind shattered in that instant, its heart failed and the wolf slumped in my hand. I obtained what I needed to know, and I felt no remorse for my actions. Though a pawn it was only, it served them and thereby became guilty in my mind. Death was for it a welcome punishment and easily one well earned.

With the force of a garrison of cannon, I stormed out to the edge of town, carrying on my back the carcass of the deceased animal. I would use it to show my resolve (in a manner of speaking), and that I was no longer a boy with whom trifling may be made. With resolute will and strength of body that came from beyond the grave I marched past the dismal homes.

I saw only red, and I knew the way. I stomped past the vineyards that I knew so well, where the grapes would in time make fine fruit and spirit to hale the heart of men. The same vineyards where I often purchased the wine consumed with our nightly meals. Past the bread maker, whom only days ago presented me with the loaf that Grandfather and I ate with our supper, the same meal wherein we discussed the days events that seemed so long ago, but were not so long in reality. The same meal we shared after I had to burn Grandfather's books--his beautiful tomes of knowledge.

So long ago? Not hardly, but that is how it seemed. So much had happened since then. So much pain and suffering. True, there was some good as well: Juliana and I are one, and no greater good can I imagine. And it is from this union that I called to her from my soul and I would come unto her, and release her from her captives like a great storm with thunder, rage, and lighting. I will wash away them from her path, leave clean the mind and spirit, and with my anger, righteous and true, I will make them suffer if they dared touch her.

The very thought propelled me forward with haste and strength. No! They would not harm her, nor our precious life she carried. My child would not know their dark caress. My child will not come into a world where they exist. Their hatred for life, the turmoil they bring--these things I will sweep away so that the better part of me that passed into her and produced this child will come in due time to a world where love exists unbounded. Their kind I will not suffer.

I felt such unending vigor within me, my quest impelled me onward. Past the hill and stream, and on into the cemetery where the Doctor and Madame lay in perpetual rest--and beyond that, not long, not far, the vision in my head shown me the way: the wolf's mind lay bore open and I knew the path, past the bridge, into the steps and through the door. I knew where they brooded, and would be for not very much longer.

The cemetery loomed in my clouded vision. It lay in a field in a valley in a meadow near water and woods. It was here the wolf would not come into the light, it was here that Juliana and I first truly came into contact. It was here I learned her touch and her mind. So long ago, it seemed.

Onward, down the slight incline I went. Past the first few stones, but only by steps, it was then that I heard them: the voices.

Like a trickle from a shallow stream they started, tickling

slightly at my ears. But as I focused more, I heard them clearly--the voices of children, many younger than I when they died. Their souls called out, pulled out towards me from their graves. I heard them, and my pace slowed as I was in wonderment and shock at what they said.

"...He hurt me!..." cried one, the voice of a girl perhaps as young as six.

"Who?" instinctively I answered.

"...The Doctor!..." came the reply.

I went on, forward and away. I turned my head to watch my path, and found myself treading on the grave of another: a soldier who long ago lost what war it was he fought. I stepped off it quick and gingerly and I apologized.

"It's alright," echoed his reply, "I've been far worse off! I don't think they ever found my head!"

I turned again, and I heard the girl again, this time louder, almost as if she was following close behind me.

"...You must tell the others! The Doctor touches you! We don't like it!..."

I didn't like the connotation, "Touches?" I asked.

"...Yes, not nice! He offered us candies..."

Was this possibly true? Were the dead telling me that which I had never known about this man--my friend, my mentor--that he had a predilection toward children in a way I could not stomach? That no normal, sane person would? Was he so filthy, but so well mannered, as to hide it for his whole life?

I shook my head. That which I knew about the Doctor wouldn't tell me this to be true. He was a good man, struck down by evil. The child had to be wrong.

Continuing forward, I turned. I would not listen to her, even though her voice rang in my ears like a church bell a thousand times too small.

Madame's grave was still fresh. I saw it. I looked, she had no stone yet, which is a pity--such a fine woman, albeit paranoid at times, but kind as the best of man can be. As I approached, I heard her moaning in sadness.

"Madame?"

"...Locarno!... My boy!..." Her voice wavered in and out of audibility, confounded by her sobbing.

"Yes, ma'am," I replied, "It is I."

"Tell Edouard... Tell him... Please!..." She was partially lost in the aether.

"Tell him what, Madame? I cannot hear!"

"...Tell him, my love... forever..."

Indeed, what I had thought before was in fact true: she loved him for all time: forever. Like Juliana and I, yet older. More so was her love, I think, for their relationship stretched on for decades. I could not imagine a love so strong as that--to bind her here until Grandfather comes. She would wait for him, here, in repose, until he came. She explained to me--as much as she was able--that she had always loved him and was afraid in life to admit it.

I had not the heart to tell her he was gone. My spirit lightened at this sign of love. The dark red of my anger slowly gave way to pink and lighter crimson.

"I will, Madame," and on I went, with her background of sobbing like a drumbeat sending me forward.

"...Locarno?..." Came a cry. I stopped.

It was the Doctor. I was near him, and could feel him.

"Yes, sir?"

"...Oh, that is you! Splendid!..." Ever himself, even now, even in death. "Have you heard them? The children?"

"Yes...they tell me things, Doctor, about you..."

He responded in a powerful yell, "Pay them no heed!"

The wind blew when he spoke. From where the breeze came, I do not know. I felt the cold of the wind, it didn't bother me, but I knew what powerful emotion it took to bring it from beyond--if indeed that is its origin.

Much calmer, almost in an instant he retorted, "They lie. Children cannot be trusted!"

I stood dumbfounded a moment. Then came "You believe me, don't you, my boy?"

I questioned him, but his deceit was clear, and he offered up nothing more than a pitiful attempt to hide his guilt.

Now I felt no misdeed from the girl when she spoke as I did from the Doctor. It seems his skillful lies worked more potently in life than here in death. I looked at his stone, a cross with his name engraved upon it. I didn't like it. Christ would not approve of his actions, and neither did I.

I remembered what the black tome said about the dead: they lay, but most assuredly they lie to further what goals in life they held dear, and some cannot be trusted. It was the Doctor who lied, I felt it, I knew it, I know now this man deserved no remorse either. Children, left in his care, were brought to sorrow. This I could not abide.

My anger returned. One does not touch children in unkind or unseemly manner! Everything within me was red, and all about me was tumult of mists of anger and agony.

"No, it is you who lie!" I spoke for those little ones whose spirits walked up to me, all pointing fingers at him--accusing him, mocking him. All with sad with faces of anger, despair, and hopelessness.

The little girl, she stood at my side, silent now, judging him with eyes from beyond death.

"The children are here, Doctor. Tell me again how they lie?"

I could feel their spirits, there was no falsehood within them; but the Doctor was very much quite the opposite.

I felt his fear grow. Though dead, it isn't certain that spirits cannot war among themselves. Were they stronger they could tear at his spiritual flesh, but slight they were--just as they were as they died-- and they were ineffectual against his girth and strength. As we age, our spirits grow too, along with our bodies; and these children, dead early, had no chance to grow strong as he had done. Deprived of life, their spirits were frozen like ice at that moment in time.

As they raged against him, he fought back; and I stood in awe at the sight of the genuine anger and hate these young ones brought forth. They set forth their cries of anguish and screamed, letting loose into the air the terrible things he did to them--things I will not repeat-- things that only I heard. Things so disgusting that to hear them injured my soul, and I, though no longer living, wept tears from dead eyes. This man, I trusted, counted friend, loved as family--but my trust was misplaced, my family made depraved because of it; my heart ached and was broken as I swept him away from me, the secret place in my heart where his memory lived was emptied and I would hold him dear no more.

I did not stop them in their fury; but as they tired, they faded from view, and the Doctor remained, steadfast he said he was innocent but offered nothing more.

In my anger, I cursed him: if these things were true, if he was this monster, let Hell drag away his spirit and let him become the prey for things more vicious than children possessed of righteous anger.

He stood--well, as much as a greatly diminished spirit can possibly stand--and looked at me. I raised my hand in a fist, and struck his stone, shattering it; and it fell. He bowed his head and faded from view: a guilty man's punishment brought forth from a judge and peer.

I stormed off, filled with new desire to be away from this scene: there is no serenity in death; and only Juliana's life mattered now. But as I left the cemetery, I turned once, and I saw her there--the girl--who looked at me and smiled, and clapped as only a child filled with glee could, and she faded away as her laughter of joy echoed across the meadow and took root in hidden places throughout the glen.

There are many kinds of compasses: some physical, pointing to the North, navigating sailors on the waters of the world; some are moral, telling men the difference between good and evil, and informing us that just because we can do something, that does not mean that we should attempt it; and then there is the compass which leads me to Juliana--a spiritual one. It links us, binds us, through the woven filaments of fate, to one another. I am the Navigator on her sea; she is my refuge, my port, a lighthouse against a darkened and dangerous sky to whom I may cling in comfort.

It is this that grants me the knowledge of where she is. Surely, I know she is with them, and they are with her; and I know the path to their very door as it was laid open before my eyes when I took the knowledge from the animal I carry. But whereas I should feel her more strongly as I approach, I do not. It is as if there is a mighty fog between us, obscuring her from me, taunting me. I sense she is within this fog; I feel her warmth, but there is no disturbance within it, therefore were it not for the knowledge I possess of their precise location I would be lost like a ship at sea with no sail or rudder.

I do not like the sensation I feel. She is clearly in danger, but she does not seem to pay the terror much heed. Though she knows she is captive (I sense it), there is this all-pervasive mist about her mind, and this worries me greatly. I must make haste!

Within the hour, I am approaching the low-lying foothills that stretch on to the horizon; and there, nestled within them is the very place to which I am inexorably drawn, the destination I violently shook from the wolf, the location where she is held from me: the Abbey of Saint Cyrillus.

Here, setting broodingly and piously in the hillside, the abbey was the oft destination for Simm. It was this place (alone in all the world) that gave him solace of mind and spirit. This was, in all manner of speaking, Simm's second home, and the source of his strongest held beliefs.

Having walked this distance before many times, I knew that I was coming close to the abbey, but I had not thought that this was in fact the location to which I was ultimately headed. My visions showed natural-earth landmarks, trees, rocks, protrusions in the landscape. The animal never cared at all for the accomplishments of the architects and builders: it was the land, its home and mother that was the true measure used for finding his way.

On a small hilltop, I stood looking at the impressive monolith of a building in the distance. I saw the door at the side. Hard wood, deep, and ancient. It was to this location I was drawn, and perhaps to the dungeons underneath. This is where Juliana was, and even though I was quite near now, the strength of her mind was to me no more potent in than before. The haze almost seemed stronger.

Down the hillside I went, boldly and with strength, my tunic flapping with my passing. Beyond trees, bush, and shrub; around leftover stones and stumps I made my way up to the very door and I looked at it as the dark wood shown heavily in the mid-morning sun. I knew that beyond this portal fate was waiting, enemies eternal, strong, potent, and powerful were on guard and may even know of my approaching. Even so, now was the time for action; for they dared to touch her, this I know, this I felt, and this I could not allow.

With a very mighty throw, I cast the wolf carcass to, and through, the door, removing it from its ancient hinges, blowing it like a bent and battered leaf down the hallway. The dead animal was lucky, for with this action its entrails and a large amount of blood was scattered in violent arcs of crimson in all directions; bones broke and tore through its flesh and it landed in a crash onto the floor, leaving foul offal like a butcher gone mad had slaughtered a calf; and as the lock shattered and fell from the frame, I stepped through from the light into the darkness. It was a reversal of when the wolf refused to come for us in the field and would not step into the light of day. I from the light went willingly into the dark; but I did not falter, would not whimper, and did not balk at the invisible division that delineates the known from the unknown.

Stepping in, I was prepared. My arrival was dramatic, loud, and meant to show them resolve; however, it left me known to them, and they came prepared.

Just as I stepped in, I instinctively ducked, and well that I did, for purposefully swung at my head was a pole-ax, which narrowly missed me but impacted the wall to my right, taking a large chunk of limestone and mold, smashing it to the ground.

My eyes automatically adjusted to the darkness, and through my red-haze of anger I could see him who wielded the ax: Tall, mean, feral, with the upturned nose of his hideous kind. I could smell him: that terrible wasted smell that nearly dropped me the first time I encountered it. Though it burned my eyes and senses, it was not as strong, and I found myself easily able to counter it with my cold, hard focus.

Just as the blade hit the wall I reached out, grabbing the beast by the muzzle. It let out a scream, a little one, but its yell became more of a choking bubble like the sounds of a man drowning as I wrenched the jaw down in a twisting motion. There was a sickening sound of bone snapping; and just when the creature's maw lay fully open and broken (and utterly useless) and its eyes flared at me in amazement and unfathomable pain, I was to darken the light of those hunter's eyes. Even before it could react or run I grabbed a large chunk of hair from its head and forced the back of his skull onto the wall.

I felt his skull splinter, and he slumped down in a pile like laundry in a bag, and the pole-ax fell like a broom, clattering onto the carved stone floor. He was not destroyed, as an undead he was already not living; but it would take quite a while for him to recover, if indeed he had the ability to do so at all. Watching as he fell, his red *Dies Irae* robe fluttered like a flag of a fallen nation, even though to me it was a forever of blissful revenge, it was only the briefest possible moment in reality. Oh, how I wish I could live in this moment of his defeat for days!

Such was not to be, and I turned and gazed in reality for the first time at the room which this unfortunate had guarded so poorly. It was merely a storage room, lit by torches, some of which were in need of replacing, there were large high columns equally spaced in two rows which supported the ceiling, which of course was the floor of the rooms above.

Toward the far end was a large wooden table, capable of seating perhaps a dozen, with high back chairs. There was no linen on the planks, and there were no cups or plates either. Surrounding this, stacked neatly, were various boxes of indeterminate size, here and there straw poked out from a few, clearly used as a packing material for whatever cargo they contained.

The air was dank, wet, and musky; I could smell dirt, mold, dust and mildew. It was the most sickening scent the world had to offer up. There was no scent of lavender or rose, or other things which I enjoy; but since I am no conquering general, and no palms were laid before me upon which I could tread, I paid the stench no heed for I had a new fixation with which to occupy myself.

Beyond the empty table, standing before another similarly sized and shaped door, were three men in dirty red robes, with piercing eyes and vampire features. A stench of death came from them; and before them stood another of their kind, garbed in a robe of red and ermine like that of ancient kings. He stood, looking, watching, and wondering. With his beady eyes, and upturned nose, he stepped slightly into the torchlight, raised his hands and applauded like one might do when viewing at the opera a performance of banality and lack of finesse; a bored clap, slow and ponderous, mocking and yet appeasing to the performer.

He was their master and commander, and it was to him that all the hell that had transpired was to be blamed; and with all my hate within me, I raised a hand back at him, pointing my bloodied finger, and spoke disgusting words, all manner of vile things that I could conjure, and imagery of a terribly dark fate that I wished to unleash upon his unsuspecting flesh.

As my diatribe was mid-stream, their leader's face turned to scorn, and he bid me, angrily, to stop as he stepped forward.

"You dare defile this House of God with your filth?"

He spoke as a man who was possessed of real, true, faith would should a person step forward and overturn an altar. Needless to say, I found it ironic that he would think me depraved when it was he who found himself that which he now condemned. I reacted as such.

"You do not command me!" I broke his next utterance, and I quickly continued with "Bring me the girl, now! Or you shall all be damned!"

He contorted his face into a cruel mockery of my anger, simultaneously dismissed my words and spoke what had to be lies.

"Fool! You do not know what it is that you face! We are not damned, rather the righteousness of God is with us!"

He stepped forward again, and now was parallel with the table, and appeared on the left of it, from my point of view.

"Ha!" I laughed, "Righteous? You and your ilk? Abominations!"

I stepped forward as well, to show that he could not approach and thereby frighten me.

"Wrong, mortal! Man is unworthy, so we bring him down from his once lofty perch. Your kind God has abandoned you for your sins!"

He spoke with absolute disdain for humanity. One could see when he spoke of our kind that it left a terrible taste in his mouth, figuratively, of course, considering he was a foul-mouthed, bloodsucking vampire: a demon, in essence, was preaching to me about redemption from sin. Amusing thought though it was, I continued.

"You feed on inferior cattle." I smirked.

His reply was terse, coarse, and deeply held, "We benefit from your destruction only to hasten it for ourselves."

It was clear *Dies Irae* not only wanted the destruction of man, but of all things, including themselves. They held themselves unworthy as well.

"Then throw yourselves into a fire."

This all was a distraction. I stepped forward again.

"Bring me the girl!" My voice became more emphatic with each syllable I spoke.

I did not believe that my anger could be so palpable. It wasn't that I just saw red, I felt it, and I exuded red. The color was part of me, the hue surrounded me, permeated me from within and from without. My eyes flamed with it. I had never been possessed of such vitriol. Never before was I, even when faced with the worst I had previously encountered, been so absolutely flush with rage. I do not know what it was that came over me to make such my feelings, other than love for Juliana; but it seemed almost out of step with reality, I was nearly beyond all control. All I knew was they had dared take her, she was mine, and they would be made to return her to me, unharmed, or the price they shall pay would be most dire. This was my only thought.

"The woman?" He spoke almost calmly, "You are quite fixated with her, aren't you? She is quite lovely, and we have enjoyed her presence greatly..."

He turned slightly to his cohorts and completed his thoughts. "...Have we not?..."

The men behind him smirked and laughed, their hideous voices were raucous and unkempt, indicating that they were in agreement with what was said. I knew this was not something I would be long in pondering the meaning of, as I didn't quite fully get their intent.

"She is of no true consequence to us. Bring her."

He turned back to me and smiled a wicked smile, from ear to ear, showing his unnaturally sharp teeth. It was as if his face tore open then, exposing a beast within: he was an animal wearing the pelt of a man.

One of his undead coterie in the rear opened the door behind where they stood, stepped in to the room behind, disappearing but for a moment only, then returned forward, bringing Juliana by her arm. She was upright, walking, but definitely was not herself.

Her face was fixed, almost paralytic, gazing off into nothing. I could feel her, even from this distance, but she was not altogether there. It was if her spirit and mind were hidden away, while only her body, like a shadow of a former self, remained. She shuffled rather than walked, as if she was mimicking the actions of walking, but did not know how to perform them herself without control from outside. That ineffable fog that surrounded her mind halted her thinking and acting in any way independent of forces from outside.

She was pale; the touch of sunlight that made her a golden light bronze was no more to be seen. Anemia had set in. Her hair, once radiant and almost glowing, was now dull, dimmed, like a candle showing only a glimpse of the previous glory of its flame; and now had gained a slight streak of silver.

Along her arms, and on the sides of her neck, where part of her dress had been torn away exposing far too much skin, there were many, many markings: the signs of something that had been feeding. Like suckers from an octopus, leaving rings, or perhaps round bites of a creature having small teeth, with torn scabs where the blood had been pulled to the surface like a leech. She had been made a meal for them.

Their leader brought her forth toward the table. I was shocked at her appearance and called her by name.

"Juliana!" But there was no reply.

His eyes never left her, but he spoke directly to me.

"Juliana?" He sighed, "So that's her name. She would not tell us. Defiant to the end."

He pawed at her cheek. Seeing his hand on her made my skin crawl. I wished to leap to action, but could not. She was in danger and I stood hopeless and helpless in my rage.

"Isn't she lovely? So precious...so precious."

I tensed up; I was aching inside, my mind raced. I wanted to grab her and run, but didn't know how I would accomplish this miracle with him so close.

"All we wanted to do was make her our queen," he quipped.

He let go, and she stood firm and unmoving; he stepped back just slightly, and removed his magnificent robe, clasp and all, and placed it on her shoulders. She looked very much like how my daydream made her, in the ermine and red, she looked very much regal, even now, to me. But I knew that dream as no more.

Then with that, he turned to me and spoke words that ran through me like a knife, words I will not soon grow to forget.

"And perhaps make your child one of us!" He touched her abdomen as he did so.

His final words echoed through the lightly lit chamber, "But you know all about seeing her as a queen, don't you?"

Her mind had been laid bare before him! He probed, and she was unable to resist, and succumbed all to his whim. He knew everything about her, down to the very last element, and therefore knew something of me as well.

In that moment I felt fear. Fear for her, fear for myself, and fear that what I must now do endangered her more so than anything I can possibly imagine.

But it was the imagined (or I think it so) voice of my child that urged me to action, calling to me, echoing to me the desires of the weak to the strong: protect and defend.

I looked at him, and he back at me; and any semblance of control I might have had was now destroyed. I screamed, and I lost a form of consciousness that the thinking man has, and charged into battle to Juliana's side. I was pure instinct; fear was non-existent.

Things happened so quickly then, I scarcely remember I grabbed her about the waist, fancy robe and all. One of the three disgusting creatures came forward with a torch. He set my left arm to blaze. Though I barely felt it, I screamed, and he fell back in terror. Their leader withdrew at my assault, sending curses that were meaningless. I think my bravery was truly something unforeseen.

A sword was drawn. I felt pain in my side. We turned together, and with great speed in the blink of an eye I was at the door.

Words were exchanged between them, "Let them go, he shall not return."

As I flew down the hills away with my prize, she was still not of right mind, so I held her tightly. Her mind was warped by them, and I did not know what I would do but to escape.

With speed that no animal could match we flew home. His parting words were correct: I would not return, for she was too valuable to me. I loved her, and I would do that which they demanded in their letter, I would flee, and her with me, and *Dies Irae* I would leave to their own devices.

Let them be damned.

In due time, we arrived home. I forced open the door with my foot, and gingerly carried Juliana across the threshold.

Stepping in, I made a mental call, and in response the fire in the hearth re-ignited, all the candles burst into flame--first blue, then turning white, and finally becoming the familiar warm yellow-orange-red, replacing in moments the light blue glow that emanated from my bedroom (where my soul resided) that flowed into the rest of the home.

Carefully, I came into my room, and placed her pale but unmoving and limp body on my bed. Her eyes were still fixed, staring off into space, seeing nothing, reacting to naught. She felt cold, but she was alive, and in time the warmth would return to her. I would see to it.

I brushed her hair from her face and was briefly reminded of his hands on her, but I suppressed my anger. Not here, not now. No, here, now, there must be no rage, no fight, nothing must come between my duty to her--to nurture her back from this place--wherever she was mentally now, I must find the way to call her back to me.

Not certain what I must do, I sat and pondered what next I should--or perhaps must--do. Oh, if only Grandfather were here.

As I thought about him, I remembered that we never

reclaimed his body. This is something I must address, but later. Not now. Not here. She must be my primary concern.

I was scarcely able to think, I needed my focus to return. That's when I felt it call to me, the phial.

I turned and gazed at its beauty once more, in a marvel. My soul, there, in a jar, sang to me in hues of white and blue. I pulled it from the shelf, bringing it close to me, it filled my sight. Close to my eyes, I felt even a little warmth come from it. I felt giddy.

Honestly, I do not know how long I stared into it, it may have been hours. I'm not sure. All I know is my standing there, staring into its beauty was interrupted by a voice in my head calling her name.

"Juliana..." It called.

Not in query, but as a reminder of my duty, my oath, my love, my wife.

But I paid it no heed, for the call of my soul was stronger; and I felt here a bliss that the waking world could not provide. All I needed was here, in my hand, in my eyes, and the outside meant nothing for it and I were one and there could be no better place in creation for me to be except here, now, with it, and the world could fade into fallen glory for all I cared.

"Juliana..." The voice emphasized the matter to me, she was all and I must focus.

However my willpower was seemingly sapped, distracted by the glowing orb in my fist. Moving, turning, pulling, wanting, needing, craving, touching, haunting, beguiling, caressing, teasing, touching, swirling, wishing, swaying, starving, singing. I was there with it, in the glass, and it with me outside. We were one being, separated by only a thin wall of substance made by the machinations of man. I could do without it being in the way, between my soul and I--I should smash this glass and reclaim my soul, be reborn and live with Juliana again!

I raised it in my hand high, and was prepared to shatter the phial as my soul called to me to end this nightmare of separation and become the *Man-That-I-Was*.

"You must save Juliana!" Again, and more forcefully, almost angrily, in my mind the voice was strong, and with this third call it paid for all my folly, and snapped me out of my daze.

I woke then, instantly. The pull on my mind was gone, and Juliana was again foremost in my thoughts. I put the phial back on the shelf, its pull would not dissuade me from my love, my duty, my wife; and I turned to her with an almost fully formed plan in mind. I would use that which I had on the messenger wolf: to crawl into her mind and undo that which had been done. But I would not use force as I had with the animal, no; I would be gentile and only probe, learn, and not push any issue. I could not, nor would not, dare to cause such injury as I had to the beast. Whereas it was destroyed by my power, Juliana must be preserved and coaxed back to the fore from wherever she has been set.

Drawing near to her, I sat and took her hand. Still she was cold, even now in the fullness of the sun that shone high in the sky, with the power of its rays pouring through the window and onto her; and she did not react in any way to my loving caress. Her pale fleshy fingers intertwined in my dead hand, but they showed no love as they had before.

As I closed my fingers about hers, my knuckles gave a creaking sound that, though light, echoed in my chamber. This gave way to me fully seeing the state I was in.

My arm and part of my body had been badly burned by the torches used against me. My tunic was mostly destroyed, the flames long burned out, and my skin underneath and along my arm was burned and blackened. There was no pain, and the disfigurement was mostly only on the surface, but the bare bone shown through in a part near the elbow.

This would not do, I will not awaken her with me in this state, it would be liable to cause her further grief--and that is not my intent. Such a sight as I am now would cause horror to her, and it must be remedied.

Knowing that medical prowess was beyond me, and that as

one that no longer held life within, it would be fruitless at best to try traditional preparations, I turned to my magic. Releasing her hand, I pulled away my tunic, and then truly saw the extent of what had transpired.

Beneath my rags there was a huge gash where the sword had slashed. I could see my entrails. My left arm from wrist to near shoulder was blackened as soot, bone was visible. My previous wound in my stomach, which had been so carefully poultice-bound by Juliana was not healed, and looked far worse than I imagined. The sight was dreadful, and was it not for the fact that I was held together by powers I cannot comprehend, I would definitely be dead. Each and every wound was surely lethal in their own right.

Amazingly, I found the lack of pain I felt to be disconcerting and worrisome. Surely, a man in such shape, even one made animate by powers of dark magic, should feel something. But as I sat and poked at my own gaping chest, I soon found it worthwhile to be without such festering issue. Pain would only make things far worse.

I called forth with my mind, and brought out from within a wave like water, starting as a ripple might in a puddle at one's feet, growing slowly until it was like a tide from the seas; it coursed outward to my extremities, and reflected back inward. I watched as my gut slowly healed, albeit imperfectly. My arm re-grew a semblance of skin over the protrusions, and muscle and sinew retied itself underneath; and my chest that had been gashed open sutured itself leaving a wicked looking scar running across like a broad river made swollen by a flood.

Though I wished to return my arm to a bloom approximating living flesh, I could not. I tried to do so for nearly an hour, but no further would it come from the boot-black color it had absorbed from the fire that singed it. Functional it was, but unpleasing to the eye it would be, apparently, forever.

That would have to serve; for now I turned to Juliana. Leaning forward, I kissed her cheek carefully, and whispered to her that I would awaken her, do not give in to fear, for I am here; and I swore to her--in the name of all things holy, honest, trust-worthy, and true that I will not see her harmed again.

"Let us begin."

Then I turned her face toward me slowly, and gazed into her listless, perfect eyes, and I began to push my mind against hers as the hours of the afternoon faded away and the world melted into the cool blue of evening as my soul played imperceptible music to us as it sat in a jar on a shelf overlooking us like a lighthouse on a cliff supervises a stormy sea.

People may be surprised to learn that fog is a mystical, magical thing. It isn't just morning dew rising like a cloud from the ground; but rather, it is something all together different: it is part physical, and part spiritual.

The fog that you see is not all there is to it; and some old pagan tales tell that it is actually woven like a cloth and is made by faeries or elves. It exists in both places, the physical world and the spiritual, simultaneously: one substance occupying two places at once. It is, without a doubt, one of the most beautiful things in the entire world.

But the foggy-mist that obscures Juliana's mind from the outside is not like the fog we see in the morning light, rising delicately to be burned away by the warm morning's rays. No, this was indeed purposefully woven, or rather built, like a labyrinth, stone upon stone, to keep her in the dark--to hide her from the outside: this was something deep and dreary. When my mind pushed against it, I was able to dissipate it where I touched.

To her, I must take the place of the fiery sun; and thereby burn away that which hid her mind from reality.

But the fog would react, slowly, filling in the void where I pressed on. Like a blanket, wet, cold, dismal, and oppressive. It wrapped, warped, folded in on itself; it was almost breathing, appeasing itself, strands wandering here and there. The paths that it took in her mind were manifold--her mind was as if there were a thousand cobblestone streets leading in all directions, but only one was the true path, all of which were identical, and none gave any indication as to which one to take, nor where it would lead, if it even lead somewhere else at all. The mind that sculpted this nightmare was ancient and evil, and by my interaction with it I hoped I learned much, perhaps instinctively, so that when I encountered it (or the architect) again, I would be able to render the designs nullified.

It took many hours to find myself inward; I would peer in deeply before I acted. I was afraid that if I pushed too hard she would succumb like the wolf before, and would have herself lost, killed, shattered--like that animal. I would press, if I felt what I can only explain as a familiar feeling or resistance, or if I noticed her react in some uncomfortable manner, I would relent--pull back--and rest her. I must not do anything that causes her even the most remote of harm.

Time was still for us; the outside world faded into nothing. I was in her mind, and her mind was around me. I could feel her, sense her, nearly taste and smell her, but she was not to be found--so well was the hiding.

There were currents, fast and slow, in her mind, and I would ride them like a leaf floats on a stream, to many secret and hidden areas of her conscious and unconscious thought; and there, when I came to rest, would begin anew. I likened this to sweeping away cobwebs from the corners of a room. A broom replaced by my will alone. The things I learned about her then--still when I dwell upon them--floor me in awe.

Long ago, she noticed me before I even knew her. She was always watching me, her dreams, even from youth, guided her toward me.

At some random time in her past, her destiny was chosen--by

her--to intertwine with mine. I saw a glimpse of her memories, a fleeting thought, of her playing when very young calling herself Queen Juliana, and of her father who asked who was her king, she replied simply and in it-will-be-so fashion, "Locarno, of course!"

There was no corresponding memory of what her father may have said in response. I did not know if he approved of this determination of hers. Regardless of what he may have thought, there were many such thoughts as this, of she and I together in her mind. And it is from this the shared-vision was transported to me, how I do not know, nor shall I ever learn that secret, I believe.

Perhaps love is its own magic: a power unto the world beyond even my beloved sorcery. If her father disapproved of me, it was not recorded or mentioned. As far as I had roamed in her mind I never saw such a memory. Juliana is a strong woman, a force of nature in her own right; headstrong, steadfast, and her own counsel does she keep, and when a decision is rendered it is held-fast and she remains resolute.

I would come to rely on this strength, just as Grandfather had tried, to keep her safe and sane while I toiled at the long work of rebuilding the bridge of her mind across the chasm that had been delved which separated her from me. There were times when I need push with vigor, and I feared for her frailty, but she did not falter, and for this I was grateful.

But even as I dug, burned, and rebuilt, I felt a presence that hovered around me: A mind, not Juliana's, and certainly not my own.

It watched, learned, saw, understood, but remained hidden, silent, and of it I knew only that it approved of what I was doing. I know this because when I needed rest a wall was built, holding back the gloom and fog; retaining and preventing a reclaiming of her landscape of the mind: a mighty embankment holding back the all-devouring gossamer curtain of forgetfulness. Great and powerful it was in this regard. When I rested, I would dwell there, sitting, attempting to commune with it, but it remained silent but very much present.

Silent it was, but only until I asked it if it were who I thought it must be: my child. Only then did it answer; and only at that time did it choose appear before me.

Like a vision in human form, transparent and translucent, with a light all its own that ensued from within. It approached from one of the myriad streets and came toward me. It stopped, stood, and looked with large brown eyes and long dark hair flowing in the breeze of currents that Juliana's mind generated; with a smile large, bright, and filled with wonder of youth it spoke.

"I am, father."

Her voice echoed about the stones at our feet, rebounded, returned, diminished and was amplified. It filled the air about us.

There it was, as I came to stand before it: the vision of my unborn child, my daughter. Lovely as her mother, yet darker in tone. Though I would not come to hold her in my arms for many months she stood there before me and I approached.

First with outstretched, timid hands, we touched, and then embraced. Though she was slight of build, and not made of flesh (and neither was I in this place, the confines of my love's mind), she was warm and I felt her and I knew then that soon she would be with us, and wherever she might be, that place was home.

She smiled as I held her, and with eyes closed her warmth burned away the mists of Juliana's mind like lightning and fire. Because of the resemblance, and to honor Juliana's mother, I knew my daughter would be likewise named Luciana.

After what seemed to be a century's long embrace, we parted, and I looked upon the young adult features of my daughter not-yet-born. I could tell from within there was great power and hope, yet despair; and I knew that she, too, had been touched (if that can be a term to use) by the feedings from those foul-mouthed, blood-sucking servants of evil.

"Luciana, I fear for you."

She knew my mind as I spoke those words, and her countenance changed slightly, and she showed some sadness.

"There is nothing to fear for me, father; I am well. From them I was able to hide, somewhat. You need worry more about mother."

She was correct in that assertion, but still I felt within her a Stygian pull of unknown origin.

"Mother fears for her brother, whom she lost, and it is partly this that keeps her in the dark, though she does not know why."

As I contemplated this briefly, Luciana interjected further.

"Though those beasts came to know me with their touch, I came in turn to know them as well; and as my memories, such as they are, was open to them, their memories and knowledge opened unto me as well."

It was in this way that they are vulnerable. What luck it was that we had a child, then; for without her hidden, secret knowledge I would not know the revelations she next shared with me.

"But what they truly desired was knowledge of you, knowledge they could not find, for it was hidden well."

"How was she able to withstand them? Hidden, where, and how?" I asked.

"By me," she answered.

"Within myself I took it as a thief might; and I hid it there, and they could not see it, for I put my mind from them and they thought me of no value."

One could see she was dejected by their lack of concern for her, but she gained the upper hand upon them and thereby showed she was of extreme worth. When this thought crossed her mind, she let loose a glimmering smile.

Speaking again, she said, "Simm was sent away for his failures. To a place they call 'The Citadel,' from whence their kind comes. His was a duty exchanged: do for them the task of destroying his own family, and receive membership in their brotherhood."

As I stood dumbfounded, she showed me the visions of what it was in the vampire's mind, as she saw them, or as she was able to recall; and here it was I came to know, and see, how it was that Simm willingly joined their cause of annihilation, and his price for admittance was the death of his mother, father, and sister.

Then Luciana explained such was the love he had for his sister, he intervened and she was spared; but his failure meant he would be punished, and so he was now away.

"He was chosen, and he chose them; for their mindset were similar from the beginning. His was the call of their summons."

It was Simm who brought this upon us all. The Doom of Simm into which we all were made to flail without mercy. I cringed at the thought that one of our own kind would turn against us, leaving us to our own peril; but it must be so--some must destroy and some build--and it is from those mere distinctions that good and evil can be discerned.

Mostly what visions she showed were of Juliana in exquisite pain. The feedings, and there were a great many, are no trifle, and though as each individual fed only shallowly, there were many of them; and the combined effect was troubling, maddening, terrible, and brought silence to a soul that laughed prior, and forged a frown from sadness upon a brow of love.

Juliana's screams echoed throughout these visions, and it was only the weaving of the hell-born mist that silenced them--and it was this same mist that was responsible for keeping her alive. Partly the mist was her own, and some from their mesmerizing.

A blessing in the worst possible disguise.

The vision she showed faded; she knew no more, and nothing else of the Citadel, and none of their further plans. I looked to her eyes, deep as dark cavernous pools, and saw no malice there. What darkness I felt must have been from their nefarious feeding, or of my own bringing, and I felt at ease.

"It will be difficult to awaken her," Luciana continued. "But if we do not do so, and soon, she will fall and I with her."

"Fall?" I asked.

I did not like the connotation of that word. It brought back to mind the tales of Lucifer who, because of his insane pride, fell from grace, was cast from Heaven, and fell into Hell itself, wherein he was tortured for all time: the uttermost source of man's undoing.

"Yes. She will fall from this world, into the shadow of the next, and will become like them. Their curse runs deep within her, and even now she fades quickly."

"How is it you know this?" This knowledge was beyond mine, and I wished to know how it was she came to possess it.

"I simply do." Her answer was short and to the point, and she held it with mastery as one who was expert might.

"Then," I spoke in awe, "we have precious little time!"

As my words trailed off, echoing within my love's mind, Luciana called out to her mother, and wielded what seemed like the very rays of the high summer sun in her hand; and like a torch magnified and glorified a thousand times--a thousand suns combined-- she cast forth these arcs of flame and power. There was music in them, and all around them was sound.

Like a choir of viols they strung out long tunes on their filaments, and the mists burned away like cobwebs that run from a candle. She made herself a beacon with which her mother might navigate her way: a great star burning in the night of her mother's mind.

She bade me join her, and using what power I could I let forth a call of magic and sound, crying Juliana's name which reverberated off the stones, the walls, and even off of the echoes themselves.

I cried out again, "Juliana!"

The tears flowed like rivers from us both.

With a third mighty draw, I let loose again, and set my voice into the sky, and the pillars of Heaven shook, there was a magnitude of great loudness as her name was let fly into creation!

"Juliana!"

My soul on fire for her, I felt something stir upon my face. I opened my eyes, and there, as I gazed down, awakened from her mind-scape realm, Juliana looked back at me, as she ran the back of her extended hand across my cheek wiping away my tears and spoke to me of her love, and how she heard my calls, and the calls of another, and she was with me then again.

And I, Locarno, the great Lord of Death, let loose a cry of thanks to God, fell to my knees, held her, and wept tears of great gladness as my dead arms embraced her living flesh while in the distance I heard the sounds of wailing women and men.

I did not care for the outside world, only Juliana mattered. She was whole, live, sane, and awake; and I was about as jubilant as possible. But even with her now awakened from her forced mental absence, she was exhausted--being called forth from such has a great tiring effect upon the mind, and she needed rest.

Before she slumbered, though, she asked me about the other who called forth her name. In answer, I placed my hand on her abdomen, kissing it softly, and told her it was our daughter, Luciana, who was there with me.

As my dry, parched lips, pulled at her supple skin, she asked how I knew that our child was, in fact, a girl.

"A daughter?"

I explained simply that I was there, with her, held her, spoke to her, and knew her as she would one day become--a lady--and that her name was the obvious choice considering that she held such great resemblance to Juliana's mother.

With this, she smiled at me, and as I held her hand, she fell into a deep, restful slumber while mouthing the name of our unborn child.

Once she slept, I placed her hand at her side, carefully, and covered her with a blanket. She stirred a little, as she was not yet beyond the veil of rousing, but she did not awaken; and I stepped back so as to not bother her.

Then the voices began.

I call them voices because, honestly, that is what it sounds like when one's own soul speaks to them: a voice. Really, more of a chorus of thoughts, emotions, ideas, wants, needs, beliefs, desires, hates, loves, and all the emotions and thoughts that accompany them--all at once, and yet separately--calling, preening, pulling, needing my touch. A soul is not meant to be separated from the host, it is both who you are and it is not; whereas the intellect is cold, logical, the soul is warm, and sometimes burns hot like the sun. The soul is emotion; it is the Want of Man made manifest.

One would be hard pressed to deny what a soul demands, it has no control, no mind, and thinks not of possible consequences or even any outcome at all. A soul wants what it desires, and it desires it now.

It was there, on the shelf, glowing, casting shadows, becoming more vehement as I drew near. I turned to face it, and the voices called forth with great strength. I saw it, and it was all there was in my eyes. The world ceased to exist, and all else was dim. The sound, first like a bee or wasp, buzzed in my ears, then rattled my temples like a snare.

The power over me it had chimed like great bells, reverberating down my spine. Muscles clenched seemingly at random. My soul wanted me to reclaim it, to consume it, and be reborn.

I took the phial from its perch, which was warm, but the contents lied to me, telling me it was cold--it needed me--and almost as if the falsehood had become true, the phial became cold.

My spiritual essence sang of love, children, and Juliana. I could feel its whispers in my mind, weaving magic and leaving residue like melted candle wax when it pulled back from the recesses of my intellect.

It advanced, retreated, and whisked a magnificent lullaby into existence that tamed me, haunted me, swayed with me like the Eastern snakes charmed by men wielding strange flutes.

I heard my soul cry out for me, and in response my body relented and I cried the last tears the dead may have; and they were followed by dank, dark, dead blood that streamed down my face, running past the edge of my chin, and dripped onto the floor.

Calling to me, telling me I was unholy, unnatural, outside of the order of Creation--but I could repent, consume it again, and become mortal again.

"Live!" It cried to me, "Life!"

I felt wracking pains in my joints, a tightening of tendon and skin, a pulling sensation at my fingertips and, as I stood, I could tell that the skin was drying underneath. Soon it was made near taught like dried leather, with creaking sounds when my fingers bowed.

My mouth, parched, tongue swollen, then dried, all in an instant, and my eyes reflected nothing of the surroundings as they, too, turned to a dim shadow of their former self, becoming like roughly made, yet still smooth, glass: without the luster of former days.

All this could be undone if only I obeyed and drained the glass, smashing it, and reclaim all that I was.

The cold of the glass became prominent, radiating up my arm to my shoulder, across my chest, past my non-functioning heart, through my lungs, down to the pit of my stomach. My breath drew cold, like when one consumes mint; and frost beaded in the air around me and on my exposed skin.

My soul called--demanded--to me: to be one again, to be heard, to be obeyed. I could not deny the pull upon my person, frozen like ice, that it had. I was cold; colder than any time in my past--colder than the winters of my youth. Colder than the time I remembered when Grandfather and I went out to the mountains to collect a certain berry that blooms there. The memory flooded my mind, out of nowhere, and I was reminded of his smile that was warm, refreshing, invigorating;

and I felt the cold halt, and turn to melt away.

His memory, his love, this was his greatest true gift to me; not sorcery or power, or even knowledge of things arcane, nor even of his great illuminated books at which I marveled. No, it was he, my family, who was in every sense of the word, the greatest gift of all: he gave of himself.

It was love that was true, and there was no falsehood within it, no pretensions and no mockeries. Is it any wonder, then, that I was roused by the warm touch of another love: Juliana. She had awoken, and called to me again and again, and I did not answer; but her touch brought me to wake from this frozen fate.

"Did you not hear me? Did you not hear them?" She was emphatic and looked at me with eyes ablaze, motioning out the window above where she slept.

That's when I heard, fully, the dismal voices of the town crying out in torment, wails and sadness.

Together we walked to the door, and I opened it, and we stepped outside and I could see that the rooftop of the Abbey, far in the distance, was burning, and I was saddened by it, but the cries were not from there.

"Locarno!" she said, as she turned me to look to the town, "The city is burning!"

Indeed it was burning: all of it. Every rooftop, as far as the eye could see was engulfed in flames. It was a sea of fire that ran to the river, and the cries we heard were that of the survivors, who clutched to the dead--their loved ones--and moaned out in absolute sadness to the God that did not answer.

So close were the flames we could feel them and the fanning they generated made a great wind that pushed back the hairs on our heads.

As I watched I knew Hell had come to Earth. *Dies Irae*--the Day of Wrath--had begun.

It is perhaps fitting, then, that these journals survive the possible *End of All Things*. Always, at every turn, have I recorded here my thoughts, fitting or otherwise, about my life, my mind, and my craft. Perhaps, should we, as a people, continue, it will be like a warning unto whomever should peruse the pages: that what we call civilization--life, love, home, and the liberties we prize--all are fleeting moments of glory and that the whims of men or demons can bring down the lofty, crushing the heads of the innocent.

With Juliana in hand, I could see with my un-living eyes the horror that was on display before me. The burning, wrecked homes, the dead lay in pools of their own blood. Some were slain, others died from the fire or smoke, and few lived to tell the tale.

Those that had been killed had not been so by sword and shield, but by more foul things--I could tell, even at this distance--that *Dies Irae* had grown bold since my meeting with them; and that they did so because they knew I had fled, which was their desire. For once, I was willing to forgo my wants, and give in to the wishes of another, even if they were my enemy.

I pulled Juliana back inside our home, and spoke with her in rushed voice, "We're leaving!"

This was not met with a response that I expected, nor wanted. She pulled her hand from mine, and expressed her lack of willingness.

"No! We cannot!"

There were tears in her eyes then, which is understandable considering that she had been through so much, and it pained her greatly; from the loss of her family, to this fire, the murders of family, friends, and those whom she loved, being little more than a morsel for a multitude of vampires; and perhaps only God knows what the future holds in the way of tortures she might be made to endure. Yet, even now, her daunting inner strength shown through, and she became resolute; even going so far as to stomp a foot in defiance.

"What do you mean, we cannot? We must! They have come; they are here, we will flee!"

My voice rang dull in the air and was heard but ignored. Her face, so beautiful, which has been through terrible events, was still soft, and she looked at me with her eyes--eyes that pierced me to my very bones. It was as if the woman I knew that day in the field had not diminished, but rather had grown in stature, becoming more than she was even against the strains of those who would do her harm and bring calamity to the world--ruin would not daunt her.

"That is what they want! If we run, where will we go that they will not follow?"

"We will go East, or North, or South, or to the West. It does not matter, just that we are away from this place--away from them!"

The words I spoke, logical; but she, possessed of fortitude that I did not have, was adamant.

"And what then when we come to the mountains? I cannot cross them!"

"I shall carry you across, or bore through the stone with my hands to save you! I will not see you harmed by them; nor our daughter!"

Love. That is what she projected to me. She came near and

touched my chest. The soft, decaying tissue underneath nearly gave way from her press; and her fingers, by virtue of her nails alone, could have carved deep to my ribs if that was her intent, but it was not. She touched lightly, with great affection, and looked up to me and my gaze met her own.

"I love you!"

"And I you... Juliana they will not touch a hair of yours again."

Such bravado, such strength in my words; it was as if the ancient kings whose mere word was law had come back from the ages past, proclaimed the law, and it was so. I slid a finger through her hair and brushed it from the side of her face, placing it behind her ear, and looked at her and knew that I would gladly play the part of coward, fool, or knave to save her from future actions of any who would dare come forward with malignant intent.

"That is why we must go. I cannot protect you here."

That was my failure, there, in spoken form. Indeed, I was deeply afraid that if they came again, what I could do would be meaningless against their superior numbers.

She placed her arms around my neck, interlocking her fingers behind my head, slightly grasping at my unkempt hair, and smiled. It lit the room more than the sun. I stared at her in wonder and a wisp of a smile of my own, a reflection of hers, crossed my lips.

"If none stand against them, then we all fall into darkness. You alone can be our champion."

Though she was sincere, I felt weak at the prospect, I was no hero, no champion as she claimed, no savior of this, or any other, world; I felt that if I left her to fight them--how, I did not know--she would become an ever greater target for their assault, and with me away she would be doomed.

I said as much, reiterating that I must protect her. That thought brought forth a memory of Grandfather--that I was to keep her from harm--and that I would do. Even if the world may burn to cinders, I would save her above all other things.

She then gave me new pause to wonder.

"If we leave, what they have done--to me--to us, will be just the beginning; and Edouard's death will have been for nothing."

Grandfather--how I wished to have your guidance now--your great wisdom, your strong ideals, your voice, your presence. How I wish this had not come to be. How I wished I could undo time itself and roll back the sun in order to know what it is that should be done.

"Oh, Locarno! I do not know why, but I am not afraid of them anymore; it is they who should know fear."

"Fear of good men." Holding me close when she said this, "Men who know what life truly is."

She spoke again in hushed tone, "Valorous men...men such as you."

I have no valor, I am but myself. I knew that though I have some measure of strength and power now, I may not use it effectively, and they have had centuries to plot the demise of man. My trepidation must have been written upon my face, and she gave me an embrace that showed what her slight body was capable of doing when pressed. I felt her warmth radiate throughout my chest. Her hair brushed my face and ear, and she smelled of wildflowers after a morning rain. Her toned flesh rippled mine, and her love withered all despair.

"I am protected here, in these arms." With that I felt my spirits lift slightly.

"They burn our city," she said as she pulled slightly away so as to look at me with surprise, as if an idea blazoned into her mind suddenly.

"Let them burn too! Become the flame to them!"

Then she spoke three simple words. Words that sealed my decision--and their fate--and drew all of us together, bound forever entwined. Words that echoed though she barely gave them the air they needed to be heard. Words that held power over me in a way I could not deny. Not wicked, wretched power, but a force of irony and justice.

Though I wished for God to rain down his judgment upon *Dies Irae*, it would be I who would be their warden. They were emblazoned into me when she spoke them, and because of her resolve they became action and command: my Queen had returned; she had spoken, and I would obey.

"Boil their blood!"

I lofted my face from her and thought to myself that if the end comes at least God would not find me wanting when the battle-lines were drawn. I looked to my blackened arm, clenched the fist, felt no pain, and knew she was correct. I alone could do this thing, the one good amongst a range of evil.

Their *Day of Wrath* would indeed come.

This day, but the wrath would be righteous.

All this desire, strength of will, mental power, obedience--all of it--was meaningless unless I could protect Juliana and answer the all-important question: where was *Dies Irae* hiding?

The Abbey, that place which was their former enclave, was burned to the ground, just as most of the city. There were many dead, but none of them were *Dies Irae*--only townspeople. So there must be a place to which they were either headed, or had already arrived for living out in the open would not serve their purposes at all. It was then that Juliana offered the advice that would, in fact answer the question: The robe.

Yes, the robe! The very garment that was placed on Juliana-- the one I carried with her when we fled.

She held the garment to me and asked, "Can you track them with this, somehow?"

Juliana didn't understand sorcery, but she knew I could accomplish any feat given time, and time we had. I took it from her and held it tightly in my hands. The grip I had on it would have torn any other fabric; and I closed my eyes, concentrated, and pushed for a vision. In my mind, I felt the cloth and looked beyond it--to its brothers.

Each member of *Dies Irae* has a similar cloak and clasp. Each one would be unique, but they were all the same. I fixated on the one-- he who was their master. I could smell him, sense him, nearly hear him; but I needed to know where he was.

In my mind I stepped back from him, turning, taking in the sights and sounds that surrounded him, he was there, so were many others of his kind, and they were feasting on the writhing living flesh. From their mouths fell both dried and wet blood as they drove themselves like a frenzy into satiation. I saw the tables, the walls, the chambers that they all occupied, and the shackles on the walls.

But where was this place?

Further back I pulled, like refocusing a perspicillum used to view the far stars of the night sky. The walls were cold and damp. There was fire, but only in torches--there was no warmth. The stones were square and large; it would have taken at least two men to move each. Very large, and old, wooden beams ran up between the stones to (presumably) the ceiling. Thick, hard, ancient trees fell long ago to make this fortress.

My eyes snapped open. That was it! They were there at the ancient Roman outpost by the lake. Long abandoned, they were there. Even the townspeople didn't go there anymore; this place was barely what you could call a ruin, and had nothing to offer except the stones themselves. A meaningless place suddenly filled with great meaning again.

It is said that the ghosts of centurions still walked the yard, and that on cold clear nights one could hear their footsteps on the stones. I, myself, had never been there. As a matter of fact, nobody I knew, except perhaps Grandfather, ever had--but he was possessed of an insatiable mind of curiosity, and wished to see what there was and if anything of value might be learned from the short expedition. There wasn't, of course, he reported; but still he went there, which is more than I could say for anyone else, including myself, until now.

I had them. Their location was known, and now I would traverse the twenty miles or more to them and they would come to know the fear that Juliana wished to instill upon them. But alas, she required protection still, for I would not leave her alone in this place--unwatched, unguarded. No, there had to be a method of protection. The militia was gone or dead. There was no place for her to hide, and even our simple home was one of very few to remain unscathed.

Grandfather once told me one day while we were out in the nearby forest that faeries were not real, even though some of the tales of their power were true; and that one could find odd rings in the ground where mushrooms would sprout, forming an arc, and no evil thing would enter them--for the land they encircled was protected.

He called them faerie rings, and considered them holy and magical, and even though he was not in any way evil, he would not cross into one; rather, he would purposefully go around them, leaving them in peace. Perhaps this would suffice.

I stepped outside, walked a few feet, and turned, facing the open door. Juliana followed to the threshold and stopped as I silently motioned for her not to leave. Kneeling down, I grabbed a fistful of soil. It was dark, rich, and moist. It clumped in my fingers and left slight stains under my nails. It smelled as if it had great potential, if indeed soil can be said to be so.

Standing, I cast the soil down, closed my eyes and thought to myself, how does one call forth a faerie ring? They're natural things, and what I must create would be blatantly unnatural, but I must at least try. Extending my arms like a half circle toward the home, I burned a blue flame in an unbroken arc. It scorched the grasses, and they browned and withered instantly. The flames extinguished, that is where I would begin.

The circle complete, I called upon the unseen seeds that lay dormant within.

"Awaken, arise..."

Focusing on the burned line, I imagined an unbroken parade

of white mushrooms growing from the decaying plants underneath, and soon small white dots were appearing in the ground where I wished them. Pushing them to grow, even with some amazement at my own ability, they grew quickly and began to mature.

Strangely, when full and complete, these were not the white, perfect mushrooms I wished for; rather, they were brown, plain, and ugly. But the line was complete, save for a few breaks, and looked much like what I had hoped to bring forth.

I could feel from them a push, as if I was perhaps unwelcome. It was unnerving, but I was, with willpower, able to cross them freely. It was this prodding, I hoped, that would keep those beasts away and serve to protect Juliana as a surrogate during my absence. Regardless, it would have to do.

Looking up, I saw her, standing there, and wished only that when the deed was done, I could return to her and live quietly here, forever. That was a humorous idea, the concept of quiet. So long had it been that there were no disturbances--deaths--mysteries that engulfed our lives. So long, it seems.

Juliana, the girl I knew, was a woman now. You could see it in her face. No longer the care-free youth, she was very much like her mother: strong, stoic, proud. She was an angel to me, something perhaps not to be approached. Yet she was approachable, and had become my bride. And with child, no less. Our child: Daughter of a Dead Man.

I knew what I must do, but I didn't wish to be gone. I would prefer to stand here forever, looking, longing for her. But I knew my duty. Though I was no real champion, I must go off into battle against powerful foes. So I turned from her, sadly and slowly, and walked directly toward town, past the burning, smoldering homes, the lamenting and crying, and the dead and the sorrowful who cried out for help that could not come just as they also perished painfully. I, the dead walking among them, sensing their fear, their pain, their doom, took the last glimpses of their decimation, savoring it; for this pity in my heart that I felt for them would be fuel for the fire that was the desire of the end of *Dies Irae*.

Should I not return, let at least my death be worthy of the price of entry into a Heaven peopled with souls such as this. An unworthy champion I am, but the only one that can be. So with a circle of flame upon my brow, I drew upon my rage and anger, and the world fell into a deep red hue as I ran, headlong, into a battle against the Enemies of Man.

Twenty miles, for one even so fleet of foot as I, who has no diminishing of endurance, is still a ponderous distance to cover; but I did so relatively quickly, arriving there in the dismal pre-twilight of early evening. A mere four hours from when I had left Juliana, but it was a lifetime in coming.

As I looked over the ruins from a scant half mile away, it occurred to me that, perhaps, I was not only destined to meet Juliana, and become a Lich, but perhaps I was also to be that which brings an end to *Dies Irae*. It's a funny thing, destiny. One never knows if you are embroiled within its myriad plots--a Pawn of Fate, if you will--or if events are simply unfolding naturally.

Grandfather considered this Earth to be the best of all possible worlds. Maybe he was right, and that there are miracles in play to generate movement of time in order to make this world better and more golden as time goes on--that the doings of men are of no consequence--and that there is a Grand Plan in the workings. Or maybe it is that we who struggle are what make this place what it seemed to him: that good men, in good time, with good intent, doing good, have over centuries made this world a far, far better place than it would have been otherwise.

It occurs to me that there is both at play, the divine and the desires of men; and only if good men act can greater good come into being, for if they do not take heed evil will dominate the landscape and darkness will fall from the sky. There is room in this wide world for the Grand Plan and Man. And if I am Pawn or King, it matters not: I will do my duty on the board--I shall play my role.

Through the trees I slowly wandered, I did not wish to bring attention to myself as I approached. Even from here, I could see the torch lights from within--they were there, those miserable beasts. My anger was not abated, but caution I could not throw to the winds. Though it was too far past the time for planning, some measure of an idea as to how my assault must begin must come to mind--I should not--must not--engage in a single, straight forward offensive. Surely, that would be catastrophic.

But I would not have the real chance to think; as it was then I was laid upon from above.

A beast, some member of *Dies Irae*, dropped on me from one of the high trees, wailing. Landing on me, from behind, it grasped me about the chest and arms. I could feel its hot breath on my neck as I struggled to remain standing under the weight. He was nearly three times as heavy as I, and very strong--as all the undead are known to be--and his grip was one of steel, and just as cold.

I went to throw myself against the tree, hoping to dislodge him from my back. Then I felt the bite. His fang-riddled mouth clamped down on my exposed neck with ferocity. He wasn't planning on feeding, rather this was a rending action, destroying flesh underneath, he wanted my blood--and he got it.
His mouth filled with my dead blood, and it trickled from the corners, and down the front of my chest. At first he laughed in a growl, but then his disposition changed quite unexpectedly.

His arms released me, and he stumbled backwards, hands grasping at his throat. Those terrible eyes, usually flashing with great malice showed pain and anxiety.

It looked at me as some of its own previous meals--the dried and sandy blood of formerly living things--and my coagulated vitae drained from his face. Tongue lashing around, he made low howls, like an animal dying. Coughing up great spurts of dust his chest heaved and he spun as if looking for somewhere to hide--to someplace with solace--but there was none around.

Falling to one knee, he reached out to me, clenching fingers probing for my clothes. Sorrowful sounds came from within him, and then he was silent. His arms fell to the side, and he toppled over to the left. Where he fell, he disintegrated into a red mound of dust and bones. Dust that quickly blew away in the wind; and bones that cracked, shattered, and slumped, were lying bleached, surrounded by his own feral and matted fur. His eyes turned upwards and fell back into the skull, turning in accelerated time into worm-ridden pockets.

It was my blood--my long-since dead blood--that destroyed the thing. There was power there, within me, making me unworthy to them as a poison is to the living; there was no need for me to fear their touch again, for I was absolutely superior to their kind.

As I watched him disappear before me, I heard a commotion from the ruins. His final howls had been heard, and they were now alert to my presence in their midst. The door swung open and two stood there, peering out into the growing darkness. Before they could see me, I had no choice but to rush to them and attack. So much for any potential plan I might have had time to conjure.

I moved toward them with absolute speed, and when I arrived I knocked on their door with both fists, dislodging it and sending it past them into the next room. They stood in awe for a brief second, then turned and leaped into the fray.

One I caught mid strike, and I held him by the throat against the wall. While doing this, the other began to draw his sword. As I held the former, he kicked me back and I dropped him. When he hit the floor, he then quickly grabbed a torch off the wall and drew a nasty looking dagger from his belt. It oozed with black, oily residue that I could smell--and it was quite foul. Two baleful blades were extended before me.

But what could they do against me? I was, after all, dead, and their assaults would not do much. I might bleed, but that would serve no purpose. They could break bones, and that was all. As I looked at them, I saw one had a terrible scar running from behind his head to the front near his eye. I looked closer, trying to discern him because he seemed familiar, which he was. He was the one whose skull I crushed in when I came for Juliana! He lived still. Healed, save for that scar, but otherwise quite robust.

They took my pause as incentive and pressed forward. The sword swung down, which I blocked with my bare hand, holding the blade firm; the other lunged with torch toward me, attempting to set me on fire. I tightened my grip on the blade and yanked it from the hand of its master, and as my clothes met the flames from the torch I thought of cold--terrible, offensive, frigid cold.

Through my red view of rage, I turned my inner fire into external ice and it projected down my arm, into the sword, which shattered under the onslaught of the impossible chill. Then this ice-flow rushed down my chest to the place where my skin began to burn, extinguishing the fire. But this cold simply would not be quenched nor halted at my extremities, and I pressed it outward, in waves, into the room, and they felt it.

Nearby torches, yards away, froze and their fires went out. A cold wind blew from no discernible place or origin, and the vampire's spittle began to solidify on their ugly faces. Their hideous breath hung in the air as a mist. Winter had come, my winter, and it was like none other on the face of the world. That's when I saw it for the first, real time: that these dead had learned Fear.

Turning to run, to escape, they moved quickly with great speed, in a blur; and I smirked a wicked smile and laughed. A laugh that echoed through the stone halls as that part of me that was called mercy was driven out of existence.

The foul dead were here, and soon they would all be made to die.

There is, and it seems as if it always so, a great moment of despair within any measure of victory. So, too, was it with me now. Even as I gloated and laughed, things were turning quite dreadful, and quickly.

As the two tried to flee to the far end of the room, several others, including their master, entered through the doorway. He was incensed and acted imperious; and instantly rallied his wayward followers, who then turned again to face me, bolstered, no doubt, by the sudden swelling of their numbers.

From behind me came a sound of many footsteps, and I turned my head to see what the commotion may have been, only to learn that now stood behind me at least four others of their infernal kind. I was not certain, but I think one of them was a female, but I paid her hideous appearance no special heed.

Always, I kept my eye on their captain, who I knew was at least somewhat formidable; the others were less of a concern to me, other than their sheer numbers. I did not know if I could survive such an overwhelming mob. But it had come far too late for such thoughts. Now I stood, face to faces (so to speak) with what, by my quick count, was at least ten *Dies Irae*, all adorned in their red robes of death, and the stench in the room was reaching nearly physical levels. I could only ignore so much of it before the fouling of my nostrils was nearly unbearable.

I stared at their lord, and he back at me. I turned my head to the side and my neck creaked ominously. It must have been a little unnerving, the sound it made, as it echoed though the room, bouncing off the stones; but I received no reaction from any of them. That is when I knew that they, though unprepared, had been through such situations before; and for them the sounds of death were more music than maddening.

When in doubt, and when one is in possession of superior numbers, it is often a successful tactic to rush the opponent simultaneously in an attempt to subdue via force. This moment was no different. Though I was quick, they were many, and I was surrounded. When they came at me, at his grunting behest, I was quickly underneath a pile of their disgusting flesh--held, clawed, struck, and almost unable to move.

One of my hands was free, and with it I grasped the body of one of the many indeterminate foes. In a wrenching turn that nearly dislocated my shoulder I tore some flesh off my assailant, and it howled in pain. But this was to no avail. I was pinned, and all I could do was wail in anger.

I then caught a glimpse of their leader, standing tall; plucking from the thin air what appeared to be nothing. Pulling from around him and placing into his other upturned palm pieces of the air itself. And in his palm, a glowing orb of blue and green could be seen forming as he did this.

My eyes widened even as I struggled against the beasts that held me, but their numbers were nothing in comparison to what I beheld: this one knew at least something of sorcery, and what it was that he did was to prepare an obvious weapon for use. I could hear, distinctly among the commotion, the cracking and singing that came from the glowing, pale orb in his hand. It surged, pulsed, and grew as he continued.

It grew in his hand and with each and every filament of magic he added, like pulling the fluff off a dandelion, he balled more and more raw power into his palm. The light it produced soon filled a portion of the room where he stood; and that is how--through this illumination--I saw upon him the markings of Trivia.

Embellished on his wrists, winding and writhing up to his elbows, almost obscured by his terrible feral and wretched animal-like arms, the marks of that ancient goddess of witchcraft shown like fire. How that I did not see it before! His was a power truly arcane and primeval. And soon, I would be the recipient of his most unwanted gift.

As he labored, he ordered his minions to stand me, and in so doing, I became a target for him--with my arms extended as if lashed, but in truth they were only held by the impossible strength of things that should not be. I tried to exert some measure of control, thinking of fear and how earlier I made the two flee from me; but in my state of agitation, anger, and rage, I, seeing only red, was in no state to form a cohesive thought let alone a successful defense against the five or so that now held me rigid. Even my head was made to face forward by two griping hands at the sides of my face.

The others were mere support for their brothers: when I pulled or tried to turn it took several of them to keep me in check. Any fewer of them and I would come out victorious, I am quite certain. It is as if over time my strength had increased by an unknown method. If only my strength were more pronounced I might thrash them against the walls.

Like a baker pushing loaves into a fire, he unleashed the glowing orb from his hand. Slowly it started, but accelerated quickly, casting long shadows in all directions as it floated toward me as a bird in flight might, or perhaps as an arrow loosed from its bow and master's hand--straight toward my exposed torso.

He beamed with delight as it approached, and the impact itself was unlike anything I can describe. Pain? Yes, there was pain--like perhaps no other, yet it was not altogether painful, as one would expect. Heat? Indeed, there was a fire unto it which I could not explain: it burned, casting the smell of singed meat into the air, which in turn filled the lungs.

Then we saw the inner light. Coming from within me, where the ball struck, I began to glow brightly. I felt numb, not unlike when I was near a tree in my youth that was suddenly the target of a bolt of lightning from an otherwise merely cloudy day. There were cracks in my skin, out from under which came more beams of light, shooting miniature sun-rays and prismatic displays onto the walls, floor and ceiling.

They released me as I shuddered. Several of them, myself as well, looked to their commander for reassurance (in their case), and surprise (which was my demeanor), as he leaned forward in anticipation, mouth open, teeth shining, drool pooling.

And with his breathy "Yes!" there came from within me a terrible ripple, and my body, in a flash, was rendered asunder. There was a noise like thunder, and for me all then was blissfully silent. I watched as my head rolled into a corner, an eye dislodged and was held in place only by the nerve as it hung there against my cheek. Many of my ribs scattered in all directions, and more than one of the vampires now had been staked with them for they were driven with great force outward, but my bones did not appear to hamper them.

My arms were flung to the side, along with shattered shoulders, and they fell to the floor. The lower half of my body, steaming like stewed venison, fell forward, slumped, and was nothing more than meat on bones. There was a spray of viscera, blood, and smoke that filled the air.

Those that had been standing, save their master, were floored, and needed to lift themselves back onto their feet. The explosion was profound, and there was a blackened scorch on the floor where I had stood.

But I remained--that is to say, my spirit, my will, stood there still--unseen and unheard in the place I occupied before. They did not know my consciousness continued as they examined my remains--the remnants of my body--and I felt a wave come over me like a rising sun--warm and glorious.

It was then I learned my final lesson: I had been reduced in potency by my dependence upon my bones. It was both apotheosis and epiphany in one. In that very instant, I had risen within a Bodhisattva (as the Eastern texts called it); and I knew what my true nature was, what power I had, and that the fate of these sub-creatures was mine to command.

I had *Become*: my capacity was unleashed.

As I stood there, with my ephemeral body laying strewn piece-meal about, with the stench of the decay of my flesh holding court in the air, I saw them and heard them mock me as they who had been knocked to the floor laughed their terrible, gut-wrenching cackle as they rose. Even their leader, once the air cleared, and the smoke and dust settled, let loose a bit of mirth from his nauseating, upturned mouth.

The female--or perhaps I should say the one most feminine in form of them--rose and cautiously went to where my head lay in a pool of my coagulated blood. My eye, which hung there against my cheek, looked at the floor, then the walls, unseeing and dim as it swung like a pendulum from the socket when she, without fanfare, lofted it up in her palm by my jawbone, and stared into my blank, dead, expressionless face.

When my eye ceased to rock back and forth, finally hanging motionless, she too laughed. Her voice was higher in pitch than the others, and as I watched her shake in amusement, barely able to hold back real tears of joy, I came to the conclusion that, yes, this one had been a girl--a very stocky, perhaps mannish girl, but female none-the-less.

I didn't like her laugh; it was both insulting and revolting. Were I still within my skin, I am certain that it would crawl in disgust. I didn't like her hands upon me, for I knew they were foul--I could see them, with their twisted fingers that ended in claws that once were nails. And the very idea of her noxious breath raining down upon my face, coupled with those gnarled, ugly fingers that were most unlike Juliana's, which were now pawing at my cheek--understandably, my lividity was not reduced, rather enhanced, by her cold clutches--somehow, except for their sorcerous chieftain, I hated her the most.

The others nearby, picked up some of my bones as if they were battlefield souvenirs, holding them above their heads. I saw all around me, I was utterly aware of everything happening, there was none who did not have one (however so small) piece of my body in hand; and now the time to act again had come.

Calling my various body parts back to me was something of relative ease; and I chose to start with my skull, which I carefully floated out of the woman's upheld hand. She, and some others, and especially their lord, watched in bewilderment as it rose steadily from her paw, and with very direct flight came back to where I once stood.

Before me, my hips and legs were slumped on the ground; and they were made to watch as my lower body rise up on its own accord, step back, and stand into the place where my spirit called it at the same moment as when my head arrived into its proper place. Ribs flew out from bodies into which they were impaled; vertebrae shivered, clicked, and scurried across the floor before rising in due time and finding their homes within the correct, overall structure of my body.

My arms, both of which were held high as a trophy, slapped their wielders and also then, once released in shock, formed at my sides as they ought, sinking into sockets. I clenched my fists and the bones reacted as they should, and I was more-or-less whole once more.

However, there was a flaw within my sight. I was no longer seeing through my eyes, rather from behind them; and the one that hung there obstructed my view slightly as I gazed around the room. Reaching up, I grabbed my hanging eye and flung it from my face, tearing the nerve from which it was suspended. Once released it flew a short distance away and down, then bounced and splashed upon the stones, rolling under a table where it would remain unnecessary, cast aside--detritus of a former life, remnants of a shell no longer required.

Again, at their master's behest, they all came at me at once. There was a great, mixed mass--a collection--of beings then, all vying for a piece of the fracas that began anew. Some with sword, some unarmed, others used weapons of opportunity from the surroundings: chairs, table-legs, rocks, and the like. It did not matter what they brought, theirs was to be extinction without quarter.

I will not say the things I did unto them: how they were scattered and torn, destroyed in so many vicious ways (and nearly demonically) by me. Heads were smashed, some were stripped of their own flesh, and some were otherwise rendered. One could, if they were so predisposed, create a great detail of how each one was, in turn, made to suffer such immeasurable agonies at my hands in those brief moments. Time was, for me, frozen as a lake in January; and I moved about them as if they were still--statues of the like a Gorgon might petrify--and not the remotest semblance of animate beings at all.

My anger, righteous or otherwise, dependent on one's own interpretation, blinded me: the Red was omnipresent. I was both in control of my actions, which took place at a blistering pace, and likewise I was without restraint or control, as a madman might be expected. Seething, with absolute turmoil within driving me, I painted the walls with their ichor. I reveled in their wallowing demise. I felt myself feel joy at their expense as they all became little more than a rag-doll in my powerful, dominant hands--a doll that soon was drenched in fluids, blood, and death. Toys (or, perhaps other playthings) they were; and I, like a vengeful Maker, truly and in every possible sense unmade them.

They were undone; and as I alone stood before him. Their

master, with all his minions broken, slain, and destroyed, whose bodies now lay at my feet, looked at me aghast and let out a cry to the heavens. It was one of fear, sorrow, loss, and hate all combined.

I returned the gaze without fear, without sorrow, and without loss, but with equal or greater hatred. In the name of God, he cursed me; but God would not, could not, listen to the squall.

His prayers would fall upon deaf ears.

Before him I stood--a patchwork man--a tatterdemalion of flesh and bone, with pieces missing and immense gouges in my skin which lay on my frame, nearly flayed, as if it was the pelt of some animal stretched upon a drying rack. Possessed of an eyeless socket burning in the torchlight, the Red was with me, and my power was amplified, as was my hate. His howls echoed as the blood of his fellows dripped from my bony, elongated fingers, with flowing filaments of pus and the essence of their entrails draining to the floor. Here and there, it would pool, like a wedding veil--speckled droplets made lacework-art out of death and dismay.

He looked at me, and I back at him. This went on for some time, his curses to me punctuating our contest. Again, I was called unholy, and again I was insulted as an abomination. But I stood motionless before him, and he knew nothing of my mind, nor what action I may take, other than that which was presently available. Oh, how I knew he wished to see through me! Oh, to be so transparent for him.

Strongly he wished me gone, but still I remained--a pillar of bones, the Apostle of Decay--and he, to me, was nothing more than filth: a disease which had permeated the living for far too long. As we stood opposite one another, watching each possible movement for a tell-tale sign, I felt my intestines go slack and drop from one of the many holes in my abdomen, slopping to the floor. The sound thus made--wet meat on stone--would have made any man, no matter how resolute, retch in horror and possibly defecate themselves. But to me it was meaningless; my will drove me now, not this body that was once my only refuge. I needed those organs no more than the oceans need sand.

As he moved, slowly and purposefully, I countered. My eyes (or perhaps it is best to say my sight) never left him. Though I could see clearly, I did not need my physical eyes any longer. The one that rested on the floor was meaningless; it was useful to the living, but I am no longer, nor have I been for some time, counted among the retinue of life. The other eye still in my head provided no hindrance either, it was neither consequential nor of benefit: it simply was. Surely, it had gone dim and upturned, perhaps the iris was now milky-white. Potentially, it was leaking upon my exposed cheekbone--it mattered not one bit other than adding silent, testimonial terror to my countenance. Through it I could see plainly, the physicality of the thing, though opaque in form, was to me nothing and it blocked my vision no more than clear glass might when added to an open window.

It was through the eyes one can see a person's soul, and thereby judge them, it was in thus manner he was found wanting in every measure. When our gaze met, he cringed, for he found within me naught but an abyss of darkness, a neutrality he could not avoid. I was the end of all things; but within him I found even less, for it is the nature of the vampire, I know, to desire the whole of the world to sate their taste. They would feed upon all mankind, drink deep of the fruit of our veins, and drain the whole world of life, leaving the Earth without populace, and still their hunger would not know an end.

If numbers stretch onward for all time, representing life, then surely they also reach back behind us equally so, representing the opposite; and if so, then vampires are beyond the pale--beyond the values attributed--and must be counted in the immeasurable negative. Such is their hunger, that howsoever great the positive upon which they feed, there is never a balance, and they will hunger still, no matter how surfeit their meal.

He breathed deeply, with wetness around his upturned, animal nose. It glistened brightly and twitched searching for any scent. Clenched fists brought bristling to the hairs on his palms, arms, and chest. The markings of Trivia, the ancient goddess, which were blisters upon his forearms, glowed with great power as he strained. I could feel the magic he wished to unfurl, it flowed from him like rivers rushing down a mountain side.

The broken bodies of his measly followers were pushed by the force of his magic, and eddies curled around them making them slowly spin as they were tossed to the walls. My gut that spilled out and sat in a lump on the floor was unaffected by his raw display, though I do not know why.

I watched to see what it was the beast might unleash. I must have seemed impotent to him, simply standing unmoving, unbreathing. I did not even tremor in the slightest.

In a brief instant, his body shimmered and shook, but one would not be able to see from where this tribulation began, because it seemed to come from all places within him at once; and his form, once fixed and firm began to stutter and change. His hands turned black, his face turned to soot, and the disturbance he generated made it look as if there was a wind pulling him apart, pushing his features to the side, and he began to dissolve in this wind like smoke rising from a campfire.

Starting at his feet, his body became insubstantial, and began to fall away--blowing in the currents of his magical prowess. Slowly, it rose up, and then soon his legs were no more. All the while his eyes never left me, and within them I saw a glimmer of hope. He thought this was his escape.

It doesn't matter what power a man might wield on the

battlefield--he may be the greatest swordsman to ever live, or the greatest tactician alive--all may be slain should a foe of sufficient strength lay hands upon an exposed neck. This was my thought in that instant, and I lunged forward with my outstretched arm, and though he was barely a dream--little more than the smoke to which he tried to transform himself--I clenched with great power upon his neck, and it solidified at my touch.

I grasped unerringly, and forced him to the wall behind. His head rest against one of the great, dried, ancient beams that held the roof of this structure aloft, and he squirmed at my burning touch.

Holding him there, it was all so reminiscent of the wolf that came as message-bearer from him. His eyes, too, were wild and searching. His feet and limbs reformed from the mist, and he tried to alter his shape again.

While struggling with me, he sprouted wings that ended in claws, with which he tried to lacerate my body, but it was to no effect; he grew an immense lashing tail for battering, to push me away, or otherwise break my grip, but this was ignored. He tried many forms--of which I cannot know whence in his depraved mind they might have originated--and none of them shook me in my resolve. I held him fast against that beam with all my might, and struggle as he would, he could not break free.

Soon his cries of anger turned to fear, torment, and terror. He wished to be free, this once servant of the church; and I would give unto him his freedom, but not in the way as he would have desired.

Leaning forward, eye to eye, I spoke to him in the language of the priests, Latin, about his doom, which I knew he understood. It would be his end--his salvation--from the living that he wished to demolish. His was an unworthy life, one he wished to be free from, and this would be my gift to him.

"*Sicut aqua calefacta ... sic tua sanguine!*"

My Latin was never perfect, but I knew he understood my words. As his eyes widened at the intonation, I plunged my free hand deep into his body through the dried muscle and skin at his side.

He screamed. I pushed onward and up, and in the fullness of time as he and I both struggled there, with him pinned against that wall, I grabbed onto his lifeless heart, and I unleashed that which I said I would, releasing the doom that Juliana had deemed for them: fire from within, bringing a boil to his blood.

Fire rose up through his form while he wailed in exquisite pain, it flickered outward through his body onto the wood of the beam while he screamed, and the timber, too, began to burn as his face was held against it.

The flames roared, and soon he was a silent shell, unmoving, no longer struggling; but still I held him there, intent on seeing the end of this thing. I obeyed Juliana's wish, my duty done, the living who had been made to suffer were avenged; but still I would stand holding this decaying, disintegrating, disgusting body there against the wall, full of flame and death, as the world around me burned and the inferno raised up all around me until there was nothing in my hands save the few remnants of skin and the echoes of his cries in my ears.

Then, when he was naught, and the bodies of his helpers were burned as well, I stood there, in the middle of the circle of flame and pondered--had I completed my fate, my doom, my destiny? Was I then finished? And if finished, should not my broken, burned, and battered body be best left to be destroyed in this holocaust as well? What duties are yet for me to undertake? Lord, will you now take me?

I raised my head and arms to the sky, and wondered aloud, "What now?"

It was then a wall beside me collapsed, and there was a free exit out of this burning hell. I stepped out into the cool, clear air. Looking up at the twinkle of the cinders that floated about I mused that they might be stars, if only they were further away. I had been spared by Providence, as a good servant might.

Then I looked at my blackened and burned, defeated and dead body and thought I could not return to Juliana in this state. Using what power I could muster, I attempted to regenerate and heal my flesh; but this was to no effect, and I was saddened. Hours went by into the early evening as I tried numerous times, each outcome remained the same.

If I were not to return home, to her--I was lost.

And almost as if commanded, a singed, but not too badly burned, red *Dies Irae* robe floated out of the column of smoke--down toward me where it finally came to rest, landing at my feet. At least I could return hidden within its winding crimson cowl. Donning it, I trudged back through the wood, avoiding any path that might be trodden, with home, and Juliana, always (and only) in my mind.

Through a cool night sky I walked, shrouded in woods and red dyed wool. Alone in the dark, I felt no eyes upon me. For the first time in quite a while, I could say that I thought there was peace on Earth, at least for now. Though alone here in the wood, which seemed once so menacing, I still was within easy viewing of what remained of my little hamlet. Many of the dead of that place were buried now, life around me would indeed continue, even if greatly disturbed. Perhaps the very idea of normal would return, whatever that might mean.

I felt no anger within and I think, perhaps, the last of it was exhausted upon *Dies Irae*; and I felt the same quiet peace within that I felt from without. I had been spared by God, and that could mean that I had done His work well.

Even so, I still felt that I was just as that bastard labeled me: unholy, abomination, and evil. I knew I was not evil in the sense he used, but still with who I am, and what I had become, those words rang with a bit of truth; I could quite easily be the damned being as he saw me.

I looked at myself: I was in ruinous condition. No mortal man could have lived with the wounds I now wear as badges of honor and combat. I walked, briskly, yet leisurely, all the while driven on not by muscle and bone but by the sole force of my desire to do so. I did not tire, I do not breathe, and I felt no pain--or anything else at all, for that matter. Actually, I was a bit numb--a lack of working nerves will bring that condition.

But again, I was brought back to the fact that, somehow, I had been spared when easily the fires could have consumed me. I did not know if that alone would bring be to destruction, but I was certain that if God wished me so, it would be at His request I perish. Therefore, I continue on because, possibly, what duties I am to undertake are unfinished; or perhaps freedom was my reward. Difficult to tell, as the mind of the Creator is unreadable by man, so I resigned myself to this fact: I shall continue on and I shall do that which needs doing, for Juliana's sake, or my own.

Juliana--her heavenly name rebounds within the confines of my mind. What would she think of me now, as I would come to stand before her broken and far worse than she may be able to imagine. It could very well be that I will learn what it is to hear her screams in the night predicated upon my appearance.

In time I came home and found myself almost at a resistant to cross the ring of mushrooms that circled the dwelling. But I was able to push through--I was, in a very real way, already within--my soul was there. And even if it were not, Juliana was inside and I would pummel any obstacle to make my way to her. Taking pause, I stood outside the door for a long while; and I could feel the warmth from within. There was a golden glow coming from inside, and I heard the crackling of a fire. I could smell her, even from this distance, even from behind a closed and presumably bolted door--it was all so inviting. I wished to rush in and take her in my ossein arms but feared that any such startle would result in something terrible.

And so, as a gentleman might, though I was indeed no gentleman any longer--being so cadaverous--I knocked gently, rapping and calling her name to answer, and waited for whatever reply might come.

"Juliana..."

It was not long before I heard her respond by calling my name. She rushed to the door, as I would have, and unlocked it, but before she opened I warned her of what she might see.

She was unfazed, and threw open to the maximum the hinges, and there I stood, wrapped in red, wearing the hood, hiding my face in a mixture of shame, sorrow, and embarrassment. She stood looking at this form that stood before her, wide-eyed, and stumbled back a step. She could see my arms, which were blackened and missing many segments of muscle, with bone protruding. It was then, I think, she fully understood the nature of what it was that I had become.

I was afraid she would find me hideous, and command me away. I could be lost then, without her, for she was my focus, my life, my love. All there was in this world was here before me, glowing with vitality; and if she discarded me like so much refuse there would be no point in an existence.

Yes, I knew fear, real fear, in that instant. Though I did not show it externally, internally I shook with terrible thoughts and horror.

She stood there, with mouth covered, for a moment only. Then unexpectedly, drew near, pulled me inside, and embraced me fully, looking up into the hood at my face which was now a mask of Death.

"Locarno!..." she gasped.

She could see my face, and then spoke to me what was a whirlwind of fortune.

"I knew you would return! And I knew something had happened... I could tell by the glow..."

Indeed so, the gold glow which I mistook from a fire was coming from the table behind her; rather, from that which now rested on top of it: my soul. It flooded the room with a golden hue, and even the blue color of the glass could not forestall it, all was awash in light like the sun: a warm, beautiful, singing light. No longer did it call to me as it once had, rather it was whole in-and-of itself now and it was there, for all to see.

"I was afraid, and wanting to be near you, I took it from the shelf and held it. It was cool then, but then turned hot and red. The whole home was glowing in that deep color! Then... gold!"

She motioned to it, and I stood astonished.

I knew when this transformation had taken place, it was when my body was shattered, and the timing of it was obvious for all who understood.

"That's when I knew you'd come home to me!"

With that, she embraced me again, her head resting on my chest; the robe alone separated her cheek from my ribs.

Before her I knelt, holding her hands, my white knuckles overlapping her pink skin, and I kissed them. She pulled back the red hood, and looked into my face. There was within her no scorn, no hate, no sorrow save for that which she missed from when I was more living in appearance; and she, smiled down to me, and within me stirred joy.

I was home; and she, my Queen, before whom and no other would I bend and take knee, showed me her heart in love.

*   *   *

The next morning, and for days afterward, I searched for the body of Grandfather, but to no avail. This is my greatest misfortune, that I could not at any time properly bury him. I think, once the vampires had finished with him for their grizzly meal, and after I had made my escape, they simply disposed of him in some shallow place where it could not be found. Animals may have dismembered him and strewn him across the countryside. This was utterly sad, and it pained me greatly that I could not reclaim the body of my family from the last evil to pervade the valley.

Many times while out searching, I saw wolves, but within them there was not the malice they once held. They were free, as was I; and I think they thanked me, in their own special way. One stared at me from a distance, and I returned the favor. Behind him I saw little ones-- pups, and they clearly were his. I didn't recognize this particular wolf, and perhaps I was reading too much into this encounter; but he followed me, and he too was filled with what joy animals in the wild can know.

As his mate took guard over their brood, he stood between me and them, and as they disappeared into the dark wold beyond the forests, he yawned, smiled, then turned from me and ran. Since then, in this part of the world, wolves were never seen, nor heard, again.

After months of looking, Juliana and I found a simple stone--crude, dark, and very dense--upon which we chose to carve Grandfather's name. To him we would raise this as cenotaph. We placed it at the edge of the cemetery, for I did not wish to intrude into the paths of the dead who lay in rest; and as we stood there before it, she said a small benediction to his memory, while taking my hand--with her living fingers intertwining to my boney, white skeleton--and together we bowed our heads in solemnity before the marker.

It was then I felt the pull. From far away, across the mountains, I felt it. I lifted my head and looked to the East, and as if in a vision, and I saw him there: a red robed figure climbed up the side of a steep incline of a mountain, up toward a castle made of ancient stone, where a red flag flew from one of the battlements.

This figure stopped and turned as if he too felt this pull, and looking back over his shoulder, I saw him then, and he saw me: it was Simm. With his features fully formed as a vampire, he clutched in his hands parchments old and worn, under seal of black wax.

We stared at one another, over these unmentionable distances for a brief second; then he turned in anger, his breath making mist in the cold, mountain air--he turned his back to me as he climbed on toward the citadel to which he headed. I knew he was their last Scion, and in time would come to be powerful--and perhaps even lead them--he was of them. He, too, had *Become*.

Juliana felt my disturbance, and looked to me, "Is everything alright?"

I turned, breaking the vision, turning back to her, and gazed into those lovely eyes.

"It is now."

She smiled at this, and gripped my hand stronger, and her love permeated my cold hand, and I was very happy with it having done so.

And completely unbidden then a large, white, ring of mushrooms formed around us and the carved stone--Grandfather's grave would remain unmolested and untouched by evil for all time. She looked at it grow, it become ivory and potent: this was a perfection of what I tried to bring into being, but failed. I knew that this was beyond my skill.

Turning to me, without words she showed wonderment, equally silently I showed that I did not cause this ring to form. She giggled a little, for it seemed that we had been present for a living miracle yet again.

*　　　*　　　*

Nigh unto nine months from the day we lay in the field, our daughter, Luciana, was born. It was a Wednesday, and the weather made no merriment--reflecting totally the mood of our daughter as she comes into the world. She would become a dark Mistress, full of power in her own right. But that is a different tale, and long in telling, and now is not the time to record those unhappy memories.

*　　　*　　　*

It is for you, the living, that I leave these journals. So that you know that in these times of darkness that punctuate our lives: when the world is dank, brooding, or dull, that there remains magic yet amongst us. You need only see it, for I exist, and shall always Be--

Locarno

Acknowledgements:

Original artwork for the cover by Gérard de Lairesse (1640
- 1711) -- public domain.

Digital manipulation and typography by the author.

Typographical font "Aquiline Two" designed by Manfred
Klein (http://manfred-klein.ina-mar.com/) -- permission for
use not required.
Available for download at http://www.dafont.com/aquiline-
two.font

First print edition.

Memories of the Dead composed using the following
software:
Scribus version 1.4.0.rc5, compiled 18 June 2011, Build
ID: C-C-T-F-C1.10.2.
Ghostscript version 9.01

Dedications:

~~In loving memory of my late mother, who always liked a good yarn, I hope she would have liked this one.~~

~~For my wife, Tammy, whose tale this is.~~

~~And finally, to Ree Soesbee, who is not only my friend, which enough is worthy of mention, but also because I promised her long ago that I would ... and you thought I forgot! ;)~~